I0555760

Cafe Stories: Riverside's Zacatecas

By William Medina

© 2023 by William Medina

COPYRIGHT NOTICE: The text and images in this book are protected under copyright laws and may not be used in any way without the written permission of the author.

Published by Coyote Hill Press, LLC, Camano Island, WA
Layout & Design by Robin S. Hanks

First Edition, 2023

Printed in the United States

ISBN: 978-1-7358615-8-6

All rights reserved.

Cover Photo: Image of the original Zacatecas restaurant in a former Stater Bros. shopping center on University and Park Avenues in Riverside, California.

Back Cover Photo: Rendering by Rita Medina of the second Zacatecas restaurant at the corner of University Avenue and Sedgwick Avenue in Riverside, California.

Contents

Foreword

I "discovered" Zacatecas Cafe in January, 1968, at the beginning of my first quarter as a history professor at the University of California, Riverside. Sort of like Columbus supposedly "discovering" America. Zacatecas had been there for half a decade before I, like Columbus, bumped into it.

One of my new colleagues and I were talking about Riverside restaurants and he chanced to ask, "Do you like menudo?" I answered "yes." He responded, "Then you've got to go to Zacatecas Cafe with me this Saturday morning. It's the best menudo I've ever had." I did go and it was game on. My colleague was right about the menudo. Saturday mornings became menudo time with my buddies at Zacatecas.

I decided that Zacatecas was Riverside's best kept culinary secret. Except that it wasn't a Riverside secret. Zacatecas found the national spotlight.

A few years after my introduction to Zacatecas, my former Kansas City, Missouri, high school compatriot Calvin Trillin, then a leading feature writer for *The New Yorker*, chanced to come to town for a story he was writing on Riverside's Casa Blanca community. As we chatted and caught up on KC old times, Calvin off-handedly asked if I knew a restaurant called Zacatecas. I informed him that I regularly had menudo there on Saturday mornings. He countered by saying I had to try its chile rellenos, the best he had ever eaten. What could I say? Calvin had written numerous books and articles on the nation's best out-of-the-way restaurants. We went and the chile rellenos joined menudo — and later beef burritos — on my Zacatecas go-to list. A decade later Calvin would eulogize Zacatecas in his book, *Third Helpings.*

The more I went to Zacatecas, the more I became aware that this then-tiny place was more than just a restaurant. It was a community gathering spot, a destination, a legend. Political leaders and other luminaries from around the state would gather there, often having to stand in line. If you visit Riverside, make sure that Zacatecas is on your go-to list.

The restaurant opened in 1963 in a narrow location within the Stater Brothers shopping center on University Avenue. It featured four tables, an eating counter, and a jukebox. Oscar and Josefina Medina, who started the restaurant, named it after the Mexican state of Zacatecas, where Josefina was born. The state also provided the inspiration for her unique recipes, which expanded the menu from the standard American food of the diner that Zacatecas replaced. The Medinas couldn't afford child care, so their kids would hang out and help out at the cafe after school. They also watched and listened. Soon they amassed stories heard from the varied clientele — statewide and local politicians, blue collar workers, university professors, people from all walks of life — sharing tables and conversations.

Later the Medinas moved the restaurant to new locations, first in 1985 two blocks up University Avenue, later to the current site on Iowa, growing each time. When Josefina and Oscar retired, their children, Suzie, Jon, and Bill took over, taking turns managing and carrying out other duties at the restaurant. Ultimately Jon and his family became sole operators.

The other siblings moved on to other things. Suzie became involved in outreach for Riverside County Public Health. Younger brother Max, who never managed the restaurant, pursued a career as a hair stylist.

Bill, the author of *Cafe Stories*, earned a Ph.D. in history from the University of California, Riverside. All the while he also worked: teaching high school; free lancing as a writer; and devoting two multi-year stints to managing Zacatecas. He later taught at Riverside City College and San Bernardino Valley College.

Bill's historical training and writing journey ultimately came together in *Cafe Stories,* a deeply personal set of short stories inspired by his personal experiences at Zacatecas. Yet these creative recollections go well beyond being a fictional institutional history. They go to the heart and soul of the Zacatecas journey: the pursuit of dreams; the resilience of family; and the building of community. The book is a deeply-felt testament to be enjoyed and savored.

Carlos E. Cortés
Edward A. Dickson Emeritus
Professor of History
University of California, Riverside
April, 2023

Acknowledgements

First, I want to thank Jeannette Casenave, who spent count-less hours revising the manuscript. Her gentle but firm approach to editing greatly improved the writing, and I am eternally indebted to her. I also want to thank Margie Akins and Henry Vasquez, who also edited portions of my stories. Their input was extremely invaluable. Judith Auth, my friend from the "old days," helped me stay on task and offered many useful suggestions — constantly reminding me to avoid the passive voice. Suzie Medina, my sister, was my auxiliary memory whose knack for remembering details enhanced each story. I am also grateful to Richard Hanks and Robin Hanks for agreeing to publish my stories, and for making critical last-minute revisions. And last, I want to thank my wife, Corinne Medina. She not only helped edit my stories, but more importantly she gave me the quiet space to create them. From the bottom of my heart, I want to thank all of you.

Preface

Oscar and Josefina Medina opened Zacatecas Cafe in Riverside's Eastside community (a racially mixed neighborhood) in the early '60s. Back then it consisted of an eating counter, four tables and a loud jukebox. No wall separated the dining area from the kitchen. Heat from the stove spilled into the dining room and made it unbearable during the summer. The original cafe was demolished, and not yet ready to retire, my parents moved the business two blocks away. The new location, once a notorious bar, tripled the cafe's size. And, unlike the original cafe, the new cafe had air conditioning. My parents retired two years later. Since then, I, along with my siblings, Suzie, Jon and Max, have managed the business. Josefina passed away in 1996, and Oscar in 2002. My brother Jon, who inherited Josefina's love for the kitchen, has since taken over the family business. He relocated Zacatecas Cafe once more, this time to Iowa Street in Riverside where it continues to this day.

Bill, Suzie and Jon Medina

I never learned to cook. I disliked cooking and avoided kitchen duty whenever possible. As a result my stories do not reveal culinary secrets, or dwell on the joys of preparing tamales. I wrote *Cafe Stories* mainly to document the uniqueness of our family's business. When Zacatecas Cafe originally opened, it wasn't a typical Mexican restaurant, but rather a public space where people of all backgrounds gathered for a meal. Our customers consisted of homeless people, politicians, students, blue-collar folks, rednecks, left wing and right-wing ideologues, African Americans, Latinos, Whites, Hippies, artists, etc. This fusion of people, tightly packed into a dining room less than two-hundred square feet, sometimes posed an existential threat to the business. However, these daunting and chaotic episodes in the restaurant's history are what made it fascinating, and which inspired my stories.

William Medina

Charlie's Departure

Old Boise, the cafe's previous owner, had fallen and broken his hip. Forced to retire, he sold the business to my father, Oscar. However, before finalizing the sale, Old Boise made Oscar promise not to fire Charlie Carr, his old friend and longtime employee. Old Boise said Charlie was a loner. He'd die of loneliness if he didn't have the cafe. It turned out that Old Boise was right.

In 1963, when my parents bought the cafe, I'd often join in the mornings to open the cafe. I was five years old. As usual, Charlie was standing by the front door. He seemed agitated and pointed his crooked finger at the grease-stained clock hanging on the wall. "You're late," he said, haranguing my father about not being punctual. In fact, we'd arrived a little early, but Oscar didn't seem in the mood to bicker with him.

"Sorry Charlie. I forgot to set the alarm clock last night," Oscar said apologetically. I overheard him tell my mother, Josefina, that he didn't want to clash with Charlie: Oscar worried that in a fit of anger the irascible man might quit. And he didn't want to break his promise to Old Boise. Besides, Oscar had once worked at a retirement home and learned to ignore the rants of bad-tempered old men like Charlie.

Wasting no time, Charlie hurried to the storage room to get a broom and dustpan. As part of his daily routine, he swept the parking lot, picking up trash left by the hobos who congregated behind the cafe at night. I asked my mother if I could go outside and help Charlie. She reluctantly agreed but told me not to bother him. Josefina said he didn't like talking to people, especially little kids.

Armed with a straw broom, I swept. Broken glass was everywhere, and some pieces were large enough to puncture a car tire. I was mindful not to cut myself. A red wine label, holding together the broken bottle, caught my attention. It was the Thunderbird brand, a low-end wine preferred by the local winos low on cash. All this time I'd been too busy to notice Charlie standing behind me. He let out a disturbing loud roar.

"Little boy! Just what the hell do you think you're doing?" Charlie said. He yanked the broom out of my hands, and made it clear he didn't need or want my help. I cringed. No adult had ever treated me so harshly.

"But my mother said I could give you a hand," I said. "I didn't think you'd mind."

"You have no business being out here. Why aren't you in school?" Charlie lashed out. His words meshed with bitterness. I told Charlie that today was my first day of summer vacation. There was no school. He seemed unmoved by my explanation. "I'm not going to tell you again. Get the hell out of here," he hollered, pointing towards the cafe.

"Leave that boy alone," shouted a passerby who'd been watching the whole time. "Can't you see he's only trying to help." Charlie told him to mind his own business. They nearly came to blows. Without being noticed, I slipped away and went back to the cafe. Afterwards I looked outside. The stranger had left, and Charlie had returned to work.

When he finished, Charlie returned to the cafe and sat at the counter. He looked exhausted and dripped with sweat. I brought him a glass of water, which he immediately pushed aside. "Didn't I tell you to leave me alone? I'm not going to tell you again," he said, shaking his fist at me. His ongoing resentment puzzled me. After all, I'd done nothing to provoke him and didn't deserve to be treated so cruelly. I didn't want to rile Charlie any further; I left him alone.

That summer was the hottest on record. The stove's heat, which blasted directly into the dining room, was enough to melt a small glacier. Once the temperature got so high that a customer fainted from heat exhaustion. Unlike Old Boise's menu that featured cold sandwiches and coleslaw, the cafe now sold menudo, chile verde and refried beans — all requiring lengthy cooking times that exponentially ramped up the temperature inside the cafe. For Charlie, dealing with brutal heat was something new.

Despite the agonizing heat, Charlie didn't move from the counter. He watched my mother prepare an order of chorizo and eggs, which gave off a savory aroma. The chorizo crackled on the stove, spattering grease everywhere. I remembered that Charlie hadn't eaten, so I wasn't surprised when he asked me what was in the frying pan. "It's called chorizo," I said. "There's more than enough if you want to try it."

Charlie said he'd never eaten Mexican food. Josefina, who'd been listening, filled a tortilla with chorizo and handed it to Charlie. He took a small cautious bite, and then threw it on the counter. "It's too damned spicy," he exclaimed. He said he had a bleeding ulcer; chorizo would surely make him violently sick. My mother looked hurt by Charlie's refusal. He was rude and thoughtless, and he didn't even thank her.

Minutes later I heard Charlie yelling frantically. The boxes of oatmeal, which Old Boise always kept in a cabinet above the sink, were all gone. Charlie was visibly upset — on the verge of tears. "Please calm down, Charlie," Oscar pleaded. "I'll get you another box of oatmeal right away." Charlie couldn't be consoled, and he threatened to quit. It turned out that my mother had forgotten to order more oatmeal. No longer on the new menu, it had become nonessential and easily forgotten. Josefina apologized to Charlie, but he just glared at her.

"The cafe's not the same anymore," Charlie lamented, pointing out that Old Boise, in all the years he owned the cafe, always bought enough oatmeal. Shortly after, Charlie stormed out of the cafe. I asked my father why Charlie was so miserable. He said we had to be patient with Charlie; his only friend in the world had moved away, and the old cafe he'd known and loved no longer existed. It left him sad and resentful.

An hour later Charlie returned. He apologized for his behavior, and asked if he could have his job back. Oscar, smiling, put his arm around the downcast man and told him not to worry. "The job is yours for as long as you like." Charlie, crying softly, thanked Oscar.

Charlie surprised me when he sat next to me at the counter. "What's that on the grill?" he asked, pointing to the thin slices of meat.

"It's carne asada. It's steak cooked Mexican style. It's used mostly in tacos," I said. I explained that my mother squeezed lemon juice over the meat to give it a tangy flavor.

I knew Charlie was hungry; I'd heard his stomach growling since the morning. "I've never heard of it. But it smells awfully good," he remarked.

"Would you like some?" I asked. Charlie asked if there was enough. "Of course. There's plenty. Josefina always makes extra." He helped himself to the thinly sliced beef. While he ate I went to the restroom.

I returned and I found Charlie clutching his throat. His face was the color of an overripe plum: he gasped for air. Oscar, acting quickly, landed a series of hard blows to Charlie's back. I'd never seen anyone choke before and watched with dread. He could die, I thought. Finally, a chunk of meat shot out of Charlie's mouth and landed on the floor.

He looked straight at me. "God dammit!" roared Charlie, now able to talk. "Can't you see I don't have any teeth; why did you give me that crap?" I wanted to cry. How was I supposed to know he didn't any teeth? After all, the chronically grim man never smiled and barely opened his mouth when he talked.

My dad told Charlie I wasn't to blame. "You're a grown man, and should have known better," Oscar said. Charlie was inconsolable. For the second time he stormed out of the cafe. I didn't know it then, but that was the last time that I would ever see him.

Days passed and Charlie hadn't returned. Oscar said the cafe was peaceful without him and took comfort in his absence. Nonetheless, my father couldn't stop worrying. He tried calling Old Boise — he would know what to do. But the retired restaurant owner had moved to Texas to be near his family and didn't leave a number where he could be reached. Fearing something bad had happened to Charlie, Oscar and I went to his apartment a few blocks away.

Oscar knocked on the door, and even peeked through the window. No one seemed to be home. My father said maybe Charlie had moved without telling anyone. Just then Charlie's neighbor emerged from his apartment. I recognized him. It was the stranger who'd come to my rescue in the parking lot.

"Are you looking for Charlie?" he asked.

"Yes. He's my employee. He hasn't shown up for work in days, and I want to make sure he is okay," Oscar said.

"I haven't seen him either. Sometimes I don't see him for days. He's a loner and doesn't talk to anyone. Not even to me," said the neighbor, who said his name was Warren.

Oscar Medina standing behind the counter. There was no separation
between kitchen and eating counter, which made dining unbearable for
customers during the hot summer months.　　circa 1970s

"If you see Charlie please tell him to call me," Oscar said.
"It's urgent." Warren said he would. He then looked at me.

"Hey, I know you. You're the little boy from the parking lot," Warren said. He told Oscar that Charlie had been
overly harsh with me, and that he'd reprimanded the old
grouch. "We nearly came to blows!" Oscar, an overprotec-
tive parent who sometimes followed me to school to make
sure neighborhood bullies didn't bother me, was taken
aback. I'd never told him about the incident, afraid that
he'd fire Charlie or do something worse: like punch him in
the nose.

"Thanks for watching over my son," Oscar said. To show his appreciation, he invited Warren to the cafe for a free meal. "Order whatever you like. It's on the house." Warren gladly accepted and said that even though he was a gringo he loved Mexican food. He shook my father's hand and then went back inside his apartment. We returned to the cafe.

From that moment Oscar didn't mention Charlie anymore. He'd even forgotten to buy oatmeal, which he'd promised to keep on hand. Oscar told my mother that he'd made up his mind to fire Charlie. He said that Charlie had become bitter and spiteful, and that he no longer belonged at the cafe. It was for the best, he said. As it turned out, Oscar never had to fire Charlie and break his promise to Old Boise.

One morning two detectives showed up at the cafe. They had bad news: Charlie was dead. A neighbor had called the police to report a terrible stench from his apartment. According to the coroner's report, Charlie died in his sleep, probably from a stroke. Before leaving they asked if Chalie had any relatives or friends who could be notified. Oscar replied, "No, Charlie had no one."

Boss

When I turned thirteen, I was expected to work longer hours at the cafe. Even on weekends. I washed dishes and swept the floor. It was tedious backbreaking work, yet I didn't mind. I got to work with Boss, the kindest and bravest woman I'd ever met. Sadly, though, after trouncing the worst bully in the cafe's history, she had to leave and never returned.

Boss and I shared the cramped dishwashing area. It wasn't always pleasant. The large woman gave off enough body heat to warm a small house; it felt like a sauna, especially during the summer months. Double my weight, Boss could have easily crushed me. She must have sensed my apprehension. She would always say, "Don't worry Memo," I won't squash you."

On the morning of the epic fight, Josefina had sent Boss to go to the market to buy hominy, which were sold in cans. She told Boss to buy as much as she could carry. "I need hominy for the menudo," Josefina said. I asked if I could go with Boss. Although the market wasn't far, (both the market and cafe were located in a small shopping center) she'd need help with the heavy cans. Josefina said I could go, but only if Boss agreed. The hefty woman said she'd love my company. The two of us set-off.

At the market we ran into Carmen Velez, Boss' elderly neighbor. "Thanks for feeding my cats," Carmen said. She'd left town for a few days to stay with her daughter and had asked Boss to feed her beloved cats. "Did my babies behave?" Carmen asked. Boss said they constantly fought and had ripped the sofa. Carmen said not to worry since the sofa was old and thick with cat hairs that clung like barnacles. Before parting, Carmen tried to give Boss money, but she wouldn't take it.

Once inside Boss and I scoured the aisles. There were only four cans of hominy left on the shelf, and we took all of them. "They won't be enough," she grumbled. Upset that the gringo market never stocked enough hominy, Boss complained to the store manager. "Why don't you ever have enough hominy? Order more next time!" she exclaimed. He apologized and promised to double the order in the next shipment.

Before we left, Boss said I'd worked hard and deserved a treat. She reached into her purse and pulled out a wad of dollar bills. I could get anything I wanted, she said. I went straight to the candy aisle. The shelves teemed with every candy imaginable — I couldn't choose. After a few minutes I still hadn't decided. Boss, irritated, said to hurry up. I finally settled on a Hershey Bar, my favorite.

On the way back Boss abruptly stopped. She said the pain in her ankles was excruciating, and she couldn't go any further. She grimaced. "Should I go get help?" I asked. Boss didn't reply, and instead leaned on me to keep from falling. It was then I felt the enormity of her weight.

Ray, a taxi driver and a regular at the cafe, spotted us from across the street. He must have sensed something was wrong. He quickly pulled up alongside us and jumped out of the cab. "What's wrong with your leg, Boss?"

"It's my ankle. It hurts like hell," Boss said.

He told her she didn't look well, and opened the door to his cab so that she could come inside and rest. Ray looked worried. "Maybe you should go see Dr. Gram; he's just down the street. "Get in and I'll take you there."

"You're a kind man," Boss said as she climbed in the taxi. "But I only need a few minutes of rest, and then I'll be fine." Ray and I looked on as Boss massaged her thick ankles, which resembled wood pilings used to build sea walls.

"Soak your ankles in Epsom Salt when you get home tonight. It'll ease the pain," Ray suggested. He added that he had a pair of crutches at home, and she was welcome to them. Boss politely thanked him but declined his offer: she didn't want anyone to think she was a cripple. A call came over the radio. Ray excused himself, and said he had a fare waiting for him across town. Boss, ever so slowly, got out of the cab. We returned to the cafe.

Josefina cried out when she saw Boss hobbling. "Oh lord! Is your leg broken?"

Clearly annoyed by all the fuss, Boss said, "It's nothing. I'll be okay."

In a stern voice, Josefina said, "You're in no condition to work. Go home." Boss, a strong-willed woman, insisted she was fine and refused to leave, determined to finish her shift. Josefina eventually backed down, but she insisted that Boss take it easy the rest of the day. I helped Boss as much as I could in the kitchen: washing pots and pans that seemed to replicate like a virus. With plenty of aspirin, Boss eventually completed her shift. She seemed on the verge of collapse.

Josefina, who'd already left for the day, had told me to make sure Boss got home safely. I offered to walk her home, but she refused. "I'll be all right, but thanks for offering, Memo." Adding, "When I get home, I'm going to soak my feet in Epsom Salt, just like Ray said." Boss gathered her belongings and bid everyone farewell.

She was nearly out the door when Fidel entered. He was a foreman at a nearby packinghouse and a regular customer. When Fidel spotted Boss, he begged her not to leave. It was his birthday and he wanted Boss to honor him with a song. "Come on Boss — just one song. It's my birthday," begged Fidel, surrounded by friends.

Beneath Boss' gruff exterior was a stunning voice. Customers paid her to sing: the extra money helped pay the rent, she often said. Born under different circumstances, she might have performed at the Hollywood Bowl, or appeared on the Ed Sullivan Show. Instead, she used her God given talent to entertain hard-drinking men at the cafe. She told Fidel that she didn't feel well and was going home. Fidel got on his knees, begging Boss to stay. She gave in, but said she'd only sing one song.

I don't remember the tune she sang that night, but it left listeners dazed. One of Fidel's friends got teary-eyed; he quickly wiped his face so that no one noticed. Boss herself looked emotionally drained, holding on to a bar stool for support. Fidel thanked Boss. He didn't want her to stop and asked the tired woman to sing one more song. Boss wouldn't yield. She'd had enough. She was going home.

Just then Angel stormed into the cafe. He was a homeless teenager Boss had found one night rummaging through the dumpster, looking for something to eat. She felt sorry for the teen and invited him inside for a meal. Since then, Boss had been feeding Angel at the cafe. She'd grown fond of him, and she often told customers that Angel was her son. According to Boss, Angel's father threw him out of the house when he found pictures of Angel kissing a boy. With nowhere to go, he'd been sleeping in a homeless shelter.

Angel demanded to see Boss. "Where's Boss? I need to talk to her!" She'd been in the restroom and came out right away when she heard Angel's voice.

"What's wrong mijo?" Boss asked.

Angel was on the verge of tears. "I can't stand that place anymore," Angel cried out, referring to the homeless shelter where he'd been staying. He told Boss that during the night someone had tried to rob him, even though he owned nothing worth stealing. Even worse, he pointed out, were the bedbugs that bit him unmercifully. He said he wasn't going back there and preferred to sleep outdoors and take his chances. Boss hugged him and told him not to worry. From now on he could stay at her apartment.

"Thank you, Boss," Angel said. "You'll see, I won't be any trouble. I promise." Angel breathed a sigh of relief. He embraced the kind-hearted woman.

Boss, who didn't have children of her own, had become a parent by accident and quickly fell into the role of an overbearing mother. "Look at you: you're filthy, especially that shirt. Go get cleaned up." Boss said she was going next door to the thrift store to get him another shirt. Angel wanted to go with her, but she insisted that he stay. "Wait here, I'll be right back," she said. Boss told me that Angel looked starved, and to make sure he ate something. I grilled Angel a quesadilla. Angel thanked me and said one day he'd pay me back for all the free meals he'd been eating at the cafe. I told him not to worry: his tiny appetite wasn't a threat to the cafe's profits. I was curious how he managed to survive on the streets. "How do you get food if you don't have any money?" I asked. I hoped not to appear too meddlesome, but Angel didn't seem to mind my curiosity.

He spoke softly. "Before I met Boss, I mostly ate out of trash cans. But it isn't so bad as it sounds; people throw away good food all the time," he said. He added, however, that you had to be careful. "Once I got food poisoning and nearly died." Angel seemed more relaxed. I tried to imagine myself in his place. After all, he was just a few years older than me.

All this time Fidel had been leering at Angel. Fidel detested gay men, and he frequently used the slur, maricon, which in English was equivalent to faggot. He'd even taunted Angel before at the cafe, but not in Boss' presence — he knew she cared for Angel and didn't want to rankle the powerfully built woman. This time, however, Fidel was drunk and reckless. I thought my presence would discourage him, but it didn't.

The unthinkable happened. Emboldened by alcohol, Fidel began cursing at Angel. "You pinche maricon! We don't want your kind here, so get the fuck out." He shoved Angel against wall and held him there. The bony teenager was no match for a man twice his size and didn't fight back. Fidel's friends quickly wrestled Fidel to the floor and held him down. I wanted to call the police. Marina, the cafe's newest waitress, said that would only make things worse, so I didn't.

Amid the mayhem, Angel and I hid in the cafe's only restroom. "We'll be safe here," Angel said. I could still here men scuffling in the dining room. Moments later I heard the back door open. Boss had returned; it was safe to come out.

Boss, surprised to see us stepping out of the restroom together, asked what was going on. She turned to me. "You'd better tell me what the two of you were doing in there." I said we were hiding from Fidel. He's drunk and he tried to beat-up Angel — he called him a maricon. Boss' face tightened. "That son of a bitch. I'll break his neck for this."

A deeply religious woman who seldom missed church, Boss asked God to forgive her for what she was about to do. She headed to the dining room. "Please Boss, don't hurt Fidel. He didn't mean it," Angel begged. She ignored his pleas and continued. We followed close behind.

Without being noticed, Boss walked up to Fidel and busted a beer bottle on his head. He instantly dropped to the floor and lay motionless. I thought the blow had killed him, but then I heard him moaning. I'd never seen so much blood, not even at the butcher shop. Fidel's friends crowded around him and tried to stop the bleeding with a towel Maria had brought. They cursed at Boss who instead of running away, stood by defiantly.

An ambulance arrived within minutes. After wrapping his head in gauze, paramedics recommended that he go to the hospital: he'd suffered a serious scalp wound that required stitches. Fidel said he felt fine and refused to go to the hospital. No one could make him, he said. Frustrated, the paramedics packed up their gear and left. After getting to his feet, Fidel left with his companions. I later heard that Fidel ended up in the hospital that night. He got eight stitches.

Oscar had been visiting friends in San Bernardino that evening. He'd missed the brawl. After hearing what had happened, he said Fidel was no longer welcome at the cafe. "If he comes back, call the police," he said. Boss apologized. Oscar told her she wasn't at fault and had nothing to worry about. Afterwards, we got busy and put everything back in order. I got stuck with the unsavory task of mopping up Fidel's blood, but I didn't complain — I was just glad the night was nearly over.

Before she left Boss gave me a warm hug. She thanked me for helping Angel and said that without my help Angel could have been seriously hurt. "You're a brave boy," she said. She gathered her things and left.

Boss didn't show up for work the next day. Worried, we went to her apartment, but she wasn't there. Not even Boss' neighbor, Carmen, knew her whereabouts. Oscar contacted the police who promised to call if they found out anything. Ray had also joined the search, taking time off from his taxi job to scour the neighborhood. She'd vanished.

A week later I ran into Angel at Lincoln Park. I told him Boss had disappeared and asked him if he had seen her. He was hesitant to give out any information, but then relented. "Boss went back to Mexico," he said. Someone had shot at her apartment. She wasn't hurt, but the bullet had shattered a ceramic saint that she kept on her nightstand. "Most likely it was Fidel." Adding that Boss left town the next day. "Except for me, she didn't tell anyone." I told him to be careful. Fidel might go after him next.

Months later a letter arrived from Mexico. It was from Boss and had no return address. In it she thanked my parents for their kindness and apologized for leaving so suddenly. She wrote that she was doing well and living with relatives, and for us not to worry. Then she asked my parents to look after Angel — she'd even included a hundred-dollar bill for him. Even though Boss promised to write again, sadly, she never did.

Political Boot Camp

I'd seen his face on campaign posters all over the barrio, so it wasn't hard to spot Bob Kerr when he walked into the cafe. The white candidate was seeking a seat on the city council and wanted Oscar's support. A well-respected business owner, Oscar's endorsement would be a major boost to the candidate's campaign.

As it turned out, both men loved airplanes. During WWII Kerr was a pilot and flew B-17s. He said he'd bombed many German cities, including Dresden. He told Oscar that not a day passed that he didn't think about the war — many of his close friends didn't survive. Oscar also had ties to military aircraft. He'd worked on fighter jets before opening the cafe and could name every single part of a jet engine. For hours they talked about flaps and air turbulence, which I knew nothing about.

Before leaving, Kerr asked Oscar if he'd endorse him for city council. And, if he could put up his campaign poster. My father, without hesitation, promised to help the former pilot. He'd make sure to display it in a prominent spot where everyone could see it.

Despite my father's infatuation for the candidate, I disliked Kerr. I was only fifteen, but old enough to spot a phoney politician. To me, Kerr was just another hack politician who'd do or say anything to get elected. At campaign rallies in the barrio, he blurted phrases in Spanish and ate tacos to endear voters. But among gringos, he called Mexican immigrants law breakers and supported mass deportations. Like other white politicians, he used the cafe like a fish farm to snag Mexican votes and then he'd disappear until the next election. Over the years I'd grown to resent this charade.

His second visit was unexpected and caught me off guard. To make matters worse I'd forgotten to hang his campaign poster. I couldn't even remember where I'd left it. I frantically searched the kitchen, and found the poster under the sink, covered with water stains. Using a damp towel, I wiped-off most of the unsightly marks, but not all of them. Preoccupied talking to customers, Kerr didn't notice as I mounted his poster over the cash register. He turned and saw it.

"There's my beautiful poster!" Kerr said with great enthusiasm. "Isn't it a work of art? And so pristine." Apparently, he didn't notice the faint traces of grime that I couldn't rub off. He bragged that the posters had taken a huge bite out of campaign funds, but worth the extra cost since they looked so spectacular.

To me his sign was ordinary and uninspiring, particularly the red, white and blue lettering: "Bob Kerr A Man Of Integrity." It sorely lacked originality. Nearly every campaign poster I'd seen used similar slogans with patriotic colors. Such posters popped-up like unsightly weeds during elections, and stayed up until a strong wind carried them away.

Eager to talk to his new friend, Kerr asked if he could see Oscar. I told him my parents were in Ensenada visiting relatives and would return in a few days. The candidate looked disappointed. He'd brought photographs from his days in the military, and he'd already laid them out on the counter. I pretended to be interested. "These are great pictures. I'm sure my dad would love to see them," I said. Kerr said that he'd love to come back another day and show him.

Afterwards, Kerr returned to the task at hand: getting votes. He went from table to table, striking up conversations with customers who were polite but clearly annoyed. After all, they'd come to enjoy a meal and not to be bothered by a politician they'd never heard of. Ironically, some of the diners were Mexican immigrants: the same people he'd denounced at rallies across town. If he'd been anyone else, I would have asked him to leave, but Oscar had given him permission to campaign at the cafe.

Kerr talked to every customer. He'd even approached the tortilla delivery man, who knew little English and just nodded. He sat at the counter that faced the stove and gazed curiously at the massive pot. He asked what was cooking. I told him it was menudo.

"I've never heard of menudo," Kerr said. "What exactly is it?"

"It's a soup made with tripe, hominy, and red chile," I said. I explained that menudo was a favorite dish among Mexican people. "It is a big seller here at the cafe. Some people claim it cures hangovers." He appeared interested.

Under normal circumstances, Kerr most likely would have declined my offer. But in the midst of a political campaign, he couldn't afford to appear aloof or snobbish. For me, this was an opportunity to humiliate him in public. He'd surely gag or spit out the tripe and embarrass himself. To ensure he took the bait, I told him that Mexican people considered it rude for a guest to turn down a meal, so I advised him to eat the menudo.

"What the hell. I'll try a bowl." Almost immediately he spit it out, just as I had predicted. He said that the tripe was too slimy and hard to swallow. His face turned red, and he looked away in shame. I'd tricked him and should have felt triumphal, but instead a surge of shame took hold of me. Duping him into trying the menudo was underhanded and cruel. He could have choked as I had when I first tried eating tripe.

I took away the bowl. "Don't worry, I don't like tripe either. It makes me gag." I remarked that one had to acquire a taste for it. But Kerr insisted on finishing. This time he only ate the hominy, which he seemed to enjoy. He later apologized for not finishing and joked that he'd probably lost my vote. I replied that for a gringo he had done well.

To my surprise Kerr didn't leave. He'd regrouped and continued greeting new customers and passing out campaign literature. He now seemed less stiff and formal. Customers even laughed at his stale jokes, and some promised to vote for him. After an hour, he sat at the counter. He looked worn out and his voice was raspy from talking so much.

Moments later, Dulce, the neighborhood prostitute, walked in cafe and sat at the counter, right next to Kerr.

She was a steady customer. Everyone liked her. Even Josefina, who railed against prostitution, treated her kindly and without judgment. As usual, Dulce wore her signature short dress that showed her thick thighs — she often said that without them she couldn't pay her rent. Kerr hurriedly moved to another bar stool, away from her. I didn't blame him. After all, how would it look for a politician to be sitting next to a streetwalker?

Unfortunately, Kerr couldn't ignore Dulce without appearing rude. He introduced himself. "Hi, I'm Bob Kerr. I'm running for city council." He graciously extended his hand to Dulce who responded with a menacing glare.

"Are you a cop? You look like one," she said, pointing her finger derisively at him. Dulce disliked policemen. They routinely harassed her, and she'd been arrested several times for prostitution. Residents often complained that the police weren't doing enough to get hookers off the street, which resulted in even more arrests. Dulce kept insisting that Kerr was a cop. She said she'd seen him riding around in an unmarked car, which wasn't true.

"He's not a cop," I said, annoyed by her stubbornness. "His name is Kerr. He's running for city council, and he was just trying to get you to vote for him."

"Well, I don't vote, so he can just leave me alone," Dulce replied. I offered her something to eat, hoping that would get her attention away from Kerr. "I'm not hungry right now. I'll be back later when the cop's gone." Dulce gathered her belongings and stormed out.

Shaken by Dulce's outburst, Kerr said he didn't mean to upset my customers. I told him he wasn't to blame and apologized for Dulce's childish behavior. I said Dulce was usually polite and thoughtful, and sometimes even brought us donuts. Kerr said that he didn't blame Dulce for mistaking him for a cop. After all, he remarked, he did resemble a vice cop. His business suit, haircut, and speech all screamed cop. I laughed. Kerr stayed a while longer. He told me old war stories, especially of his bombing missions in Germany. Kerr finally left but promised to return in a few days.

Later that afternoon Father D, the local parish priest, arrived dressed in his traditional black robe. He'd brought someone with him. "I want you to meet Ron Tunney. He's a candidate for city council." Father D scolded me for not immediately shaking the candidate's hand — so I did.

"I hear you have the best Mexican food in town," Tunney said.

"I can't take credit for that. My mother does all the cooking," I replied.

"Well, it sure smells awfully good," Tunney said. "Maybe, if there's time, I'll get something to eat."

"Where's Oscar?" Father D interrupted, glancing at the back kitchen. "I want him to meet Mr. Tunney." I explained he was out of town and would be back in a few days. "Oh, what a shame." The activist priest, who'd marched with the farm workers in Delano and who disliked the police, said he wanted our family to do everything possible to help elect Tunney, who was running for city council. It was the same council seat Bob Kerr was seeking, I thought to myself.

"I'm sure my father will help him," I said. Father D reigned over his congregants with a firm hand and people seldom disobeyed him, so I didn't dare tell him that Oscar had already committed himself to Tunney's opponent.

"Tunney's a good man," insisted Father D. He said Tunney grew up in Indio and had worked in the fields during the summer and understood the needs of poor people. And more importantly, he said, Tunney could speak Spanish unlike his opponent, Bob Kerr. "Tunney doesn't need a translator. He can talk directly to the people."

While Father D extolled the virtues of his candidate, I suddenly remembered that Kerr's poster was hanging on the wall. Father D would be furious if he saw it. Luckily, he hadn't noticed. Without calling attention to myself, I quietly took it down and hid the poster in the back kitchen.

Tunney picked up a menu. "I see you have menudo," he said. "It's been years since I had a bowl."

Unlike Kerr, Tunney was familiar with Mexican food, and gladly accepted my offer of menudo. He squeezed lemon juice into the steaming bowl, adding oregano and cilantro. Like my Uncle Paco, he dumped clumps of butter into the thick soup. If eating menudo was a litmus test for politicians, Tunney passed easily. He declared that the cafe's menudo was the best in town, and suggested I figure out how to mass produce it and make a lot of money.

Meanwhile, Father D had gone to his car and returned with a Tunney campaign poster. Without asking permission, he hung it on the same nail that earlier had held Kerr's. "This is a great spot for the poster. Everybody can see it when they come in," he said, adding that Tunney was going to win, and he'd be a big plus to the community. Before leaving Tunney thanked me for the menudo and promised to do a first-rate job if elected.

I felt conflicted about the dueling campaign posters. Although I disliked Kerr's politics, I had grown fond of the gringo politician. On the other hand, I didn't dare cross Father D. After much thought I came up with a solution. Using an old bottle of Elmer's Glue, I pasted the campaign posters back-to-back. They were a perfect fit. I attached a string that made it easy to turn the poster around at a moment's notice.

My scheme unraveled from the start. Kerr had forgotten his briefcase and returned. He immediately spotted Tunney's poster. I expected him to be upset. Instead, he smiled and told me not to worry. After all, he said, playing both sides was smart and ensured the cafe got behind a winner. I later showed him how I'd glued the posters together. He said I had a knack for politics, and that I should consider running for public office one day.

Campaigning had taken its toll on Kerr. He looked exhausted, and asked if he could get something to eat. I jokingly said that he should try another bowl of menudo. He politely declined. "To be completely honest, I don't think I could ever like menudo. Are burgers on the menu?" I told him that even though the cafe specialized in Mexican food, we made the best burgers in town.

Cooking 101

On my sixteenth birthday Josefina announced it was time I learned to cook. Although I'd been helping in the kitchen for years, I never took my duties seriously. I had no plans to become a cook. Stirring pots all day in front of a hot stove didn't appeal to me. Nevertheless, Josefina said I had to learn for one day since I, along with my siblings, would inherit the cafe. Thus began my involuntary apprenticeship in the kitchen.

My first day as a cook trainee started on a Monday. Milo's Meats had just delivered five boxes of pork butts. I went straight to work, cutting the clumps of meat into bite-sized cubes — ideal for burritos. Soon animal fat covered my hands, and even got under my fingernails. And even though I'd grown up in a restaurant, famous for its pork dishes, the smell and feel of pork sickened me. It made me want to puke at times. I ran to the sink to wash off the revolting slime.

Gavino, a recently hired kitchen helper, had been watching me with amusement. "Memo, you should be used to handling meat by now," he laughed.

To him I probably seemed like a spoiled brat. After all, my family owned a restaurant and I got to eat for free whenever I wanted. He'd grown up in Tijuana in extreme poverty, often missing meals. He shrugged his shoulders and jokingly said I should put myself up for adoption and find a new family — one that didn't own a restaurant.

Josefina joined us at the cutting table. "Why aren't you guys working?" she grumbled. Actually, we'd been working all along, but that didn't matter to her. Although a warm and friendly person, my mother habitually upbraided her kitchen staff. No one was spared, not even her own children. "We have over a hundred pounds of meat to cut today, so let's get to work." Without delay, the three of us started cutting.

After a few minutes I stopped. I told Josefina that my knife was dull and needed sharpening. "This knife couldn't cut jello," I said sarcastically. Indeed, a dull knife not only was inefficient, but also dangerous. Having to press down harder, the knife could slip out of my hand and cut me. Last year I got four stiches from such an injury.

Josefina seemed annoyed by the interruption. "Let me see your knife," she said. After trying it out, she insisted that the knife was fine. She'd recently had them all sharpened. However, in order to satisfy me, Josefina reached for her old, trusted metal file and sharpened it. "Now get back to work." Gavino, who'd earlier complained about the same thing, didn't say a word: he knew better than to complain.

Two hours later we finished. Accustomed to years of grueling kitchen work, Josefina didn't show any sign of fatigue, nor did she complain. By contrast my right hand ached from holding the knife's handle for too long, and my fingers had grown stiff. Yet I didn't dare let on about my pain. Josefina would have excoriated me.

Generally, my mother didn't allow breaks, except to go to the restroom. The hard-nosed restaurant owner worked non-stop and expected the same from others. State labor laws, which mandated rest periods, didn't apply in her kitchen. All breaks were granted on a case-by-case basis — all at her discretion. I must have looked tired and deserving. When I asked for a time out, Josefina, to my surprise, said yes but told me not to take too long — that meant no more than five minutes.

Due to limited space, the cafe didn't have a designated breakroom. Employees took breaks either in the dining room or outside behind the cafe. I wanted to be alone and stepped outside, away from the clatter of plates and away from my mother's watchful eye. However, my solitude didn't last very long. Tony, who owned a small store on Park Avenue, pulled up in his grocery delivery truck. He'd been looking for me.

"Memo, you're just the person I need to see. Hector, my old helper, quit yesterday. I need a new stock boy right away. Would you be interested in the job?"

Oddly enough, in the past year, I'd been thinking about quitting the cafe. Josefina barely paid me the minimum wage, and I needed to earn more. Especially now since I'd had my eye on an old Chevy on a car lot on Market Street. "Yes," I said without hesitating, but then asked Tony if he could wait until tomorrow. I had to talk to my parents first.

"I won't be able to wait too long," he replied, and then asked me how things were going at the cafe.

I told him Josefina was teaching me to cook. "My mother says it's about time I learned this part of the business," I said. "She'll be angry if I quit."

Tony shook his head in disbelief. "You mean you grew up in the restaurant business and you're barely learning to cook?" Tony had four sons, who'd learned the grocery business at a young age. They could stock shelves and operate the cash register like seasoned professionals. But they were now grown and had moved out years ago. Since then, Tony had been hiring boys from the neighborhood to help run the store. He said the job was mine if I wanted it. He got back in his truck and left.

I'd been outside long enough and returned to the kitchen. Josefina and Gavino had already started seasoning the meat. I took my place at the table. Together, we rubbed oregano, red peppers and salt into the pork — adding vinegar as needed. We mixed vigorously for almost an hour. I was exhausted. Even Gavino, who had the stamina of a plow horse, looked tired. Afterwards we packed the meat into plastic bags and stored them in the freezer, to be used later in the week. We'd finished.

I'd decided to write down Josefina's recipes. Sitting at the counter, I jotted down a few notes in my notebook which I kept in my back pocket. Even though I had no intention of becoming a cook, I still felt an obligation to contribute to the family business by recording its trade secrets. As I wrote Josefina looked on.

"What are you doing?" she asked.

"I'm writing down the steps for seasoning the pork butts," I said. I proudly showed her my notebook and pointed to the different seasonings she'd used.

Josefina laughed mockingly. "Your little book is a waste of time."

Her dismissive attitude upset me. "I'm recording your recipes for when you retire, and we take over the business," I said.

"You can't learn to cook from a set of instructions," she said. "You have to learn by doing." Besides, she added, food never comes out the same — regardless of how closely one follows a recipe. A careless cook might add too much salt or leave the meat in the oven too long. "My kitchen isn't a factory that churns out tacos like cars." With that said, I put down my notebook and stopped taking notes. It then occurred to me that I'd never seen a measuring cup or cooking thermometer in her kitchen.

Later that day Josefina left to run errands. She'd left a pot of chile verde cooking on the cast iron stove, which over the years had turned black from baked-on hardened grease. Before leaving, she told me to stir the meat to prevent the pork from flaring up. And that under no circumstances was I to leave the stove unattended. She told Gavino to keep an eye on me, and then hurried out the door. Minutes later I heard a car honking — it was Gavino's girlfriend. Although mostly reliable, when it came to girls, Gavino was foolhardy. As he rushed out the back door, he told me that he'd be right back. I was alone.

Bill Medina cleaning the stove. The steam in the photo comes from pouring water and vinegar over a hot grill, which produced a foul odor.   circa 1971

With the burner fully turned on, it didn't take long for the pork inside the massive pot to crackle and pop. Hot grease splattered in all directions, hitting my arms and face. I turned down the flame — the danger had passed, so I thought. This was my chance to tend to the burn marks on my arms, so I bolted for the restroom located at the rear of the cafe. The cool water felt good, and I could have held my arm under that faucet all day. In fact, I'd been in the re-

32

stroom longer than I should have. I heard someone scream, "fire!"

I hurried to the kitchen and found the stove engulfed in flames. Panicked customers had fled. I joined them outside, keeping an eye on the growing flames through the window. Within minutes the fire department arrived, honking at on-lookers who blocked the cafe's entrance. Firefighters, using heavy-duty fire extinguishers, went right to work and put out the blaze.

Josefina had returned. When she saw the fire trucks, she instantly made the sign of the cross. She asked me if everyone had gotten out safely. "We're all fine. No one was hurt," I said.

"Gracias a Dios," she said, looking upwards towards heaven.

Later, I listened closely while Josefina talked to the fire captain. "Looks like someone left a pot of pork cooking on the stove and forgot about it," he said. Adding that hot grease from the pot flared-up, and then the flames quickly spread to the rest of the stove. "The fire was intense. It could have burned down the building." He recommended degreasing the old stove, which over the years had accumulated layers of hardened grease and could result in another fire. Josefina nodded and promised to do as he said. After inspecting the stove one last time the captain and his crew left.

Understandably, Josefina was angry with me, so I tried to avoid her as much as possible. After all, I shouldn't have left the stove unattended. Curiously, Josefina never asked Gavino where he was during the fire. In fact, he'd been in the parking lot sitting in his car with his girlfriend and hadn't noticed the commotion until the fire trucks arrived. If she'd known that, Josefina would have fired him.

The task of cleaning the cafe got underway. Josefina, whose anger had tapered-off, assigned me to degreasing the stove, as the fire captain had suggested. In some spots I had to use a chisel and hammer to chip away the petrified grease. Gavino got right to working, removing the fire extinguisher's yellow powder, which covered the floor and walls — the tiny particles had even gotten inside the jukebox. Josefina rinsed every plate and every piece of silverware and checked the shelves to get rid of food that had been contaminated. When we finished, the cafe looked as though the fire had never happened.

That night I stayed in my bedroom. Riddled with guilt, I considered staying at a friend's house, or even moving out permanently. But I couldn't leave right now. My dad was in the hospital and undergoing tests. Suzie was too busy with her social life to manage the cafe, and Jon was in Mexico helping my Tia Pancha on her farm and wouldn't return for a few weeks. Josefina needed me so I stayed.

The next day Tony walked into the cafe. He hadn't come to eat, but to ask me if I'd made up my mind about his recent job offer. "Have you decided yet?" Tony asked. He said he needed an answer right away. Josefina spotted us talking.

She seemed irked by Tony's presence. "Hello Antonio," she said, refusing to call him Tony because it sounded too white. "I heard you're trying to steal one of my employees," she remarked sarcastically. She already knew about Tony's job offer. Maybe Suzie had found out and told her. Josefina had her own spy network, so nothing got by her.

Tony laughed and said, "Josefina, it's time for your little bird to leave the nest. You can't keep him to yourself forever, and besides he'll earn more at my store."

"Memo can leave whenever he wants," Josefina shot back in an unpleasant tone. Tony, stunned by her reaction, apologized and said he didn't want to cause friction within the family. If that was the case, he'd hire someone else.

I stepped into the brewing fray. I wanted to prevent a serious falling-out between the two merchants, who'd known each other for many years. "Thank you for the job offer Tony, but I can't leave right now. My father's been sick, and I'm needed here at the cafe," I said. I expected Josefina, who didn't tolerate disloyalty, especially from her own children, to fire me on the spot. But she didn't.

Tony said he was disappointed but understood. He had to get back to the store, so I walked him to his car. Before leaving, in a low voice so that Josefina couldn't hear, Tony promised not to hire anyone in case I changed my mind. Apparently, despite my refusal, he had a hunch I'd accept his job offer. He'd read my mind.

My brief apprenticeship turned out to be an utter failure. My cooking skills never improved. I still burned food, and I still abhorred the scent of pork. One day I found the courage to tell Josefina the truth: I had no intention of ever taking over the family business. "It's not what I want to do with my life." Furthermore, I said, I'd decided to accept Tony's job offer — at least until I earned enough to buy a car.

I expected Josefina to be indignant. Instead, she responded with a mother's tenderness. She confessed that all along she'd known I wsn't meant for the kitchen. However, in fairness, Josefina explained, she felt obligated to give me a chance at running the business. "I didn't want you to feel passed over," she said. I told her not to worry about that. The following day I started working at Tony's Market, and within a few months I earned enough to buy my first car. Not long after Tony had a heart attack and sold the store. The new owner, capable of managing the store himself, didn't need me and I eventually returned to the cafe. Regrettably, I never learned to cook.

The Boycott

One morning Chicano militants, known as the Brown Berets, stormed into the cafe. They demanded to see my father. Their leader, Hugo Sanchez, said the Brown Berets were organizing a boycott against Coors, one of the most loved beers in the barrio. According to Hugo, the beer company donated money to racists groups that targeted Mexicans and thus was no longer welcome in the barrio. If we didn't join the boycott, he said, the Brown Berets would picket the cafe. Minutes later they all filed out.

Hugo returned two days later, but this time he came alone. He looked around and sneered when he saw the Coors neon light on the wall. "I see that you haven't gotten rid of the beer."

I was so nervous I could barely talk. "Only my parents can legally discontinue a beer," I said meekly. They were in Ensenada, I added, visiting relatives and wouldn't be back until next week. I hoped that he'd understand. Hugo rolled his eyes in disbelief.

"Call them, right now!" he demanded, pointing to the pay phone in the dining room.

"They can't be reached," I said. I explained that my relatives lived in an area that didn't have phone service. The nearest phone was a few miles away.

Hugo gave me a menacing look. "I don't believe you. If I find out you're lying, you'll be sorry." His threat wasn't to be taken lightly. The Brown Berets carried guns, and they were unafraid to use them — even against the police. I'd seen them training in an abandoned warehouse near the cafe. They marched nonstop from one end of the building to the other, all the while shouting angrily in unison. They were preparing for the revolution, which they said was coming soon.

A few hours later the Brown Berets showed up. They came in cars, trucks and even a small trailer, and took over the cafe's parking lot. Hugo, standing on a truck bed, barked orders at the men and women whom he called his soldados. They quickly set up a makeshift camp, and then formed a picket line in front of the cafe. Our family business, literally, was under siege. Customers stayed away the rest of the day. The cash register sat listless.

Tia Olga, who'd worked at the cafe since her divorce, wanted to call the police. "What they're doing is illegal," she exclaimed. Back then cops regularly ate at the cafe, and she often gave them discounts. They adored her, and on occasion she even invited her police friends to her home for dinner on weekends. In her mind, her close ties to the police entitled the cafe to extra protection.

"Please don't call the police, Tia Olga. It will only make things worse," I said. No telling what Hugo would do if patrol cars suddenly showed up.

Tia Olga promised not to call. "I'll call only if it's absolutely necessary." She offered to confront the bullies herself but said such unmannered youngsters wouldn't heed the words of an old woman. With my parents out of town, I'd have to face the militants alone. Then the boycott took a turn for the worse.

We'd run out of tortillas, which meant an unavoidable trip to the market. To get there, I'd have to walk across the shopping center's parking lot to reach the market: right through the Brown Beret encampment. For sure, I'd be spotted. Hugo and some of his people had already seen me and knew what I looked like. I was so nervous I vomited twice before leaving.

To my surprise no one recognized me as I snaked my way through the parking lot, trying my best to be inconspicuous. Not even Hugo noticed me, who was standing only a few feet away where I passed through. One of the militants, who was grilling carne asada, even asked me if I wanted something to eat. I politely declined and hurried off. Within minutes I arrived at the market. What sheer luck, I thought.

Once inside, I breathed a sigh of relief. I went straight to the tortilla rack and grabbed as many packs as I could carry. After all, I didn't want to have to come back again. As I stood in line to pay, I could see Hugo in the parking lot, giving orders to his minions who scrambled like worker bees. They seemed to be on high alert. Maybe I'd been spotted. If so, my return trip wouldn't be so easy.

I was right. Hugo appeared out of nowhere — as if he'd been waiting for me. "Hey, where do you think you're going?" Hugo shouted. He grabbed my arm and wouldn't let me go any further.

"I can't talk now," I said. "The cafe needs these tortillas right away." Hugo said he didn't care about the tortillas and asked if I'd talked to my parents. I reminded him that they were still in Ensenada, and that he'd have to wait until they returned.

Hugo looked exasperated. "Your parents and my grandpa have been friends for a long time, and I'd like to give you a break but I can't make an exception. Unless you get rid of the beer, we'll continue picketing the cafe." His grandfather, Rene, had known our family for many years. In the 1930s he worked at the Riverside Cement Plant with my grandfather. Hugo was torn between duty and friendship. With nothing else to say he stepped aside to let me pass. I safely returned to the cafe.

The following day Hugo brought reinforcements. They were even more ill-tempered than the others and itching for a fight. They marched single file along University Avenue, carrying placards that denounced Coors and the cafe. One sign read, "Don't Buy K-K-Koors Beer," an indirect reference to the Klu Klux Klan. In their eyes, our beloved cafe endorsed bigotry. Hugo's soldados yelled obscenities at our customers, who took their business elsewhere. Then, to make matters worse, the Coors truck arrived to make its weekly scheduled delivery.

I ran outside to warn the driver, but it was too late. The crowd had already converged on the truck and brought it to a complete stop. Hugo jumped on top of the cab, cursing at the bewildered driver who had no idea what was going on. Other Brown Berets joined the frenzy, throwing bottles and hitting the trailer with their signs. Seconds later the truck slowly plowed through the hostile crowd and escaped. Thankfully, no one was hurt.

Tia Olga had had enough and called the police. In minutes patrol cars blocked the parking lot exits and encircled the Brown Beret encampment, preventing anyone from leaving. Hugo, undaunted by the large police response, cursed at the uniformed officers. His bravado inspired the other Brown Berets, who defied orders to disperse and held their ground. An all-out battle seemed inevitable. Then, mysteriously, the police began withdrawing. I looked on in disbelief as they drove off.

Tia Olga, upset that the police had retreated, confronted Lieutenant Allen, who'd been eating at the cafe since it first opened. "Why didn't you arrest Hugo or any of his people?" she exclaimed, adding that the Brown Berets had attacked a delivery truck and threatened the driver. "Someone could have been killed."

Lieutenant Allen looked frustrated. "I agree. As far as I'm concerned, those troublemakers should all be in jail." However, he explained, he'd been given an order to withdraw and avoid violence at all costs — this decision had come from the mayor's office, who'd lately faced severe criticism from the Eastside community over police harassment.

A clash with the Brown Berets would have been a public relations nightmare for the city. Before leaving he apologized for not being able to do more but promised to assign a patrol car to keep a close eye on the cafe.

Not long after, the Coors plant manager called. He was furious that his driver had been attacked and threatened to call the police. I explained that the police had been called, but the delivery truck had left before the police arrived. He said the cafe wouldn't be getting any more beer until the protestors were gone. I suggested rescheduling the delivery at night after the cafe closed, but he flatly refused since he'd have to pay his driver overtime. With deliveries suspended indefinitely, Coors's time at the cafe was coming to an end.

By default, we'd joined the boycott, at least for the moment. I gave Hugo the good news and I even invited him to the cafe so that he could see for himself. He came right away and inspected the storage area. He found two unopened cases of Coors, which I had overlooked. I explained that they were my dad's private stash and not for sale. I'd get them out tonight, I promised. "I'll be back next week to check again. There'd better not be one bottle left," Hugo warned before leaving. Within an hour, the Brown Berets vacated the parking lot and I breathed a sigh of relief.

A few days later Hugo's grandfather, Rene, came to the cafe. "Where's your mom and dad?" he asked. I told him that they'd gone to Ensenada and left me in charge. Rene said it was good that my parents could rely on me and take time off to travel.

"What will it be today?" I asked.

He said that he'd been working in his yard all day and was looking forward to a cold beer. "Give me my usual," Rene said cheerfully.

A faithful Coors drinker, he'd be upset that we'd didn't have it. "Sorry, but we don't sell Coors anymore," I said. Rene, oddly, didn't ask why or make a fuss. "Would you like something else instead?"

"Give me a Coke instead," Rene said. I brought it promptly. He said he needed to talk to me and sounded serious. He said he'd heard about the boycott, and about the ruckus it caused for the business. "Tell me the truth. Did Hugo bully you into getting rid of the Coors?" He insisted that I be honest. There'd be no retaliation, he said.

Hesitant at first, I said, "Well, I guess it's true," I replied. "His friends picketed the cafe, and they even attacked the Coors truck. Things got out of hand."

"That boy's gone too far," Rene shouted, banging his fist on the counter. He apologized for Hugo's behavior and promised to talk to him. "I'll make sure he doesn't bother you again." Adding that although he admired Hugo's fight against racists gringos, he didn't have the right to treat my family so badly. He finished his drink, and told me not to worry, everything would turn out all right.

Later that week my parents returned from Ensenada. I told them about the boycott, and how the Brown Berets had picketed the cafe. Customers, under threat, refused to cross the picket line and profits nosedived. I expected Oscar, who didn't scare easily, to confront Hugo and bring back Coors. After all, Oscar was loyal to the beer brand, as were many of the cafe's customers. Moreover, he and the Coors plant manager, Roy, were close friends. On occasion Roy would give Oscar free tickets to Dodger games in Los Angeles, and he had recently sent a repairman to fix our beer cooler at no charge. If Coors returned, however, Hugo would continue picketing the cafe.

Incredibly, the Coors nightmare ended peacefully. After meeting with Hugo, Oscar agreed to purge the notorious beer. A pragmatic businessman, he realized a war with the Brown Berets was dangerous: someone might get hurt, and the picketing could bankrupt the cafe. Moreover, Oscar had other reasons for capitulating. He'd experienced racism growing up in Riverside. He often told us that public pools in Riverside only let Mexicans and blacks swim on certain days, and certain restaurants didn't welcome non-whites. He wouldn't admit it, but deep inside he knew Hugo was right. Oscar kept his word, and the cafe never sold another bottle of Coors, even after he retired.

The Mexican Hater

A few days earlier Buck had been at the cafe loudly complaining about wetbacks taking American jobs. He was drunk and combative. I refused to serve him, threatening to call the police if he didn't leave. He told me to fuck off. Minutes later two officers showed up and escorted him outside. I was surprised when they didn't arrest him. They said Buck hadn't broken any laws. They had to let him go.

On this second visit Buck sat quietly at the far end of the counter. I didn't attend to him right away, hoping he'd leave on his own. He didn't budge and instead glared menacingly at me. And even though I was now grown, his presence unnerved me. Expecting trouble once more, I grabbed a few coins from the tip jar in case I had to call the police from the pay phone in the dining room.

I took his order. "What will it be?"

"Remember me?" Buck exclaimed. He wore a dingy baseball cap and old blue jeans, the same clothes he had worn before.

"Sorry, but you don't look familiar," I said. I thought it best to feign ignorance and pretend I didn't know him. Maybe he'd forgotten.

"Bullshit! Don't lie to me," he hollered. "Look, I don't have time to waste. Just bring me something that's not too spicy."

"What about a quesadilla?" I suggested.

"What's that?" Buck asked.

"It's like a grilled cheese sandwich, but Mexican style," I said.

"That sounds safe enough. I'll take one of those qudillas," he said, mispronouncing "quesadilla." Gringo customers regularly ordered in fractured Spanish, which I'd learned to decipher.

My younger brother Jon, now old enough to work a shift by himself, got right to work. He kept an eye on the quesadilla to make sure it cooked evenly on the grill. Jon knew if it burned, Buck might make a fuss. Wary of the possible danger, Jon brought out the baseball bat he kept under the kitchen counter. He'd never used it, but it was our safety net against troublemakers. The quesadilla was now done, I took it to Buck.

In all the years at the cafe, I'd never seen anyone eat a quesadilla with utensils. Usually, people ate them with their hands like a pizza. I got Jon's attention. "Look — he's eating with a knife and fork and cutting the quesadilla into little squares." Jon shook his head in disbelief and remarked that only a gringo would do that. Such formality was uncommon at the cafe.

I was glad when Buck finished eating. I added up his check, which came out to $9.48. He tossed a twenty-dollar bill on the counter, and said I could keep the change. "Thank you," I said, surprised he'd left such a generous tip.

"Enjoy it, amigo!" he said. "Never forget that a white man gave you a ten-dollar tip." I despised his condescending tone, and wanted to throw the money in his face but didn't dare. Before he left Buck tipped his hat. Not out of respect but in a demeaning manner. I never wanted to see him again. Fate decided otherwise.

A few weeks later Buck returned. Unlike the first time, he appeared sober and reticent. He'd brought his wife, Evelyn. She tightly clung to his arm and looked about nervously. I didn't blame her. In the late evenings the cafe reeked of cigarette smoke and draft beer, and overworked men. She belonged at the Mission Inn where fine wines and filet mignon were served to well-dressed guests. I showed them to a table near the jukebox.

"Welcome," I said. I placed a bowl of chips and salsa on their table.

"Hey," replied Buck. He snatched the menus from my hand and handed one to Evelyn. I read out loud the daily specials posted on the wall, but Buck ignored me. Instead, they both studied their menus like lost tourists looking at a map. Obviously, they needed more time, so I left them alone.

When I returned to take their order, Evelyn was checking the silverware. Apparently, she didn't have faith in the A grade posted by the health department. She returned one of the forks, which she said hadn't been washed properly. To me it looked clean, but I didn't argue and run the risk upsetting them.

I brought her another fork right away. "Are you ready to order?"

"What's good today?" Buck asked, tossing the menu aside.

"Try the carnitas. It's pork that has been slow-cooked," I said. "We raise the pigs ourselves. The meat is super fresh and extremely tender." I told him my father owned a small farm, and that he'd just butchered one of his prized hogs, reserved for special customers. In fact, I said, the animal had been castrated at a young age to improve the meat's quality.

Buck seemed flattered that I'd offered them our so-called special carnitas. He glanced over at Evelyn for her approval. "That will be fine," she said.

"We'll take the carnitas," Buck said. "But first bring us a cold pitcher of beer and keep them coming." I was surprised by how heartily they drank — especially Evelyn, who didn't strike me as a beer lover.

Unbeknownst to them, I'd invented the entire pig story. Although my parents did own a small farm outside of town and raised pigs, we didn't butcher them for use at the cafe. Our meat came from a local butcher shop in town which delivered fresh meat every week. I'd lied to the couple —— it was my own quiet way to get even for their rudeness. I gave Jon their order and he went right to work.

The carnitas first had to be thawed out. This added to the cooking time, and I worried Buck would complain about the long wait. To distract them, I kept bringing beer and chips, and even made them a small quesadilla in the meantime. Finally, Jon yelled out that their order was ready.

"Here are your carnitas," I said.

"It sure smells awfully good," Buck said. By now they'd consumed three pitchers of beer and seemed less edgy. In fact, Buck cracked a faint smile.

I asked if they'd like anything else. "What do you call that round flat bread you people eat?" Evelyn asked. I barely understood her; she was slurring her words.

"They're called tortillas," I replied.

"Could I have a few to go along with my dinner," she asked. I warmed up a few tortillas and brought them in a basket. She looked clueless and asked me if I could show her how to use them.

"Yes, of course," I said. "You tear the tortilla into strips and then use them to grab the food. It's a bit messy, but that's how we eat at home." Evelyn, now clearly intoxicated, struggled to pick up the meat with the tortilla. Food landed on the floor; her face and hands shone with animal fat. Embarrassed for her, I walked away. This continued for several minutes.

Buck, who'd been watching us the whole time, reached over and snatched the basket of tortillas. He told me to take them away, which I promptly did. He handed Evelyn a fork, but she threw it back at him and told him to mind his own business. She sneered at him as she continued to eat with her hands. Quarrels weren't uncommon at the cafe, especially in the evenings. However, I'd never seen a white couple fight. Evelyn had morphed into a mean drunk.

After Evelyn finished eating, she walked over to the juke-box. In a muddled voice, she read out loud the music selections, which included country music. "For The Good Times!" she cried out. "Oh, I love this song." She said it reminded her of an old sweetheart from high school. Searching through her purse, she found a quarter and dropped it in the jukebox's coin slot. The music started.

She turned to Buck and held out her arms. "Honey, I want to dance."

"You know I don't like to dance," he said. No matter how much she begged him Buck wouldn't budge from his seat. Frustrated by his stubbornness, Evelyn danced alone be-tween the tables and counter. She bumped into chairs and tables, and nearly tripped. Buck looked on helplessly as his inebriated wife humiliated him, but he didn't try to stop her. Jon and I watched with amusement.

By now Evelyn had drawn the attention of a group of Mexi-can men sitting at the counter. They were evening regulars — the beer crowd who worked at the nearby packing-house. They watched Evelyn with curiosity and no doubt wondered about the drunk gringa. After all, white women, especially inebriated ones, were unheard of at the cafe.

Ignoring her husband's calls for her to sit down, Evelyn approached the men at the counter. She could barely stand. "Will one of you fine gentlemen please dance with me?" she muttered, adding that her useless husband wouldn't mind.

Porfi, who had a reputation for being a lady's man and had learned enough English to sweet talk girls, smiled and said, "I'll dance with you. It would be my pleasure, senora." He immediately took her by her the hand. A polished dancer, Porfi spun Evelyn several times and even dipped her. Despite being intoxicated she moved quite well. I pushed the tables against the wall to make more room for them. The cafe had become a makeshift dancehall.

Cheering him on, Porfi's friends whistled and shouted. "Shake that ass baby," they screamed, which no doubt incensed Buck. Evelyn seemed to enjoy their attention and wiggled her hips for their benefit. When the music finally stopped, Evelyn, overcome with emotion, kissed Porfi on the lips. Not a quick innocent peck, but a drawn-out smooch that for a married woman had gone beyond the pale of decency.

Buck had had enough. "Goddammit, get your greaser hands off my wife," Buck roared. He pushed Porfi aside, nearly knocking him to the floor. "I'll kill you if you ever touch my wife again." Evelyn, stunned by the commotion, returned to her seat.

Despite Buck's threat, Porfi refused to back down. He wasn't going to let a jealous husband rattle him. He cursed at Buck and demanded that they go outside and settle their differences like real men. Buck, unfazed, lifted his shirt to show the pistol he had tucked away in his pants. Tragedy loomed — I had to act quickly. I got between the two men and somehow managed to coax Porfi outdoors. Jon, who'd joined us, told Porfi he could be deported or even go to jail if the police got involved. Porfi calmed down, and shortly afterwards he left with his friends.

Jon and I went back inside. Buck and Evelyn were gone and had left without paying. But I didn't care about the money. I was thrilled the incident was over, and that neither Buck nor anyone else had been hurt. Still on edge, Jon worried that Buck might return and start more trouble. "I don't think we'll ever see Buck again," I said. "His wife had kissed a Mexican in public, and for him there was no greater shame." Jon agreed.

Blanca

At first glance Blanca gave no indication of being a hustler. She was young and attractive and didn't look like someone who preyed on the unsuspecting. Even her name, Blanca, the girl with white skin, suggested purity and innocence. She turned out to be an alluring deception.

Blanca sat at the counter. "Could I please have a bottle of Diet Coke?" she asked. I told her that we only had fountain drinks. She said that was fine, but to make sure I filled the glass to the top. Blanca didn't seem in the mood for conversation, so I left her drink on the counter and walked away. Unfortunately, her solitude didn't last long, interrupted by some notorious cafe regulars whom I fondly dubbed Los Borrachos.

Most of Los Borrachos worked at Salvador's, one of many citrus packinghouses near the cafe. They were loud and brought with them the scent of citrus, grime and perspiration. It didn't take long for them to notice Blanca, whose milky white skin was impossible to ignore. They gawked at her; I didn't blame them. She was a curiosity, especially since attractive young girls seldom ventured into the cafe unescorted. Annoyed by their attention, Blanca quickly finished her soft drink and left.

Surprisingly, Blanca returned the following day. As before, she sat at the counter and ordered a Diet Coke. She'd brought a magazine filled with pictures of wedding dresses and studied each page with keen interest. Maybe she was planning her wedding, I thought. Once again, her privacy was interrupted. Melo, the dishwasher, arrived to start his shift. He spotted Blanca sitting alone at the counter.

"Hey beautiful, can I buy you a drink?" Melo asked. He wasn't good looking and possessed the charm of a jelly fish. He constantly lied about his sexual exploits, and claimed that appreciative women bought him nice clothes and always paid when they went out to eat. In his mind, he was a Casanova — a great lover. Blanca would be an easy conquest, he told me in private.

"Please, leave me alone. I'm not interested," Blanca snapped, waving him off. Melo, ignoring her firm rebuff, continued with his stale romantic one-liners that only further annoyed Blanca. I told Melo to leave her alone and to get back to work, which he grudgingly did. I wouldn't have blamed her if she'd left or thrown her drink in his face. Instead, she asked to see a menu which I promptly delivered.

Blanca studied the menu for several minutes and then returned it, insisting she wasn't hungry after all. But she didn't fool me. I'd worked long enough at the cafe to recognize a hungry look; I wanted to help. Most likely Blanca was short on funds and too proud to accept charity. To get around her pride, I lied and said a customer had just canceled an order of tacos. She could have them free of charge. The tacos, if she didn't eat them, would end up in the garbage. Blanca thanked me, and said she'd had a big lunch and couldn't stand to eat another bite.

"You don't have to eat them right now. I'll put them in a bag so you can take them home," I said. She took the tacos but insisted on paying. I told her not to be ridiculous. Afterwards, while sweeping the floor, I found the grease-soaked bag in the trash. Without me noticing, she'd eaten the tacos and discarded the bag. I thought it best to not to mention it: she'd be mortified.

Soon afterwards Los Borrachos arrived at the cafe. They weren't alone. Big Sal, who owned Salvador's, was among them. His presence always caused a stir among the boisterous drinkers. They adored him. He paid good wages and treated everyone fairly. And although he was a gringo, he could speak perfect Spanish, which endeared him even more to the men. He relished his celebrity status at the cafe, and often stayed late into the night.

Big Sal liked to boast. He bragged that he owned a yacht, and that he'd sailed around the world three times. His brashness would certainly turn-off Blanca, who seemed to dislike conceited men like Melo. Yet from the moment Big Sal arrived, she couldn't take her eyes off him. Her sudden interest in the well-to-do man aroused my suspicion. Maybe, all along, she'd been waiting for Big Sal. Maybe she'd heard about the wealthy packinghouse owner and found out that he frequented the cafe in the evenings. That would explain why she returned.

It didn't take long for Big Sal to step into Blanca's trap. I was standing behind the counter when he called me over. "Hey Memo, who's that good looking gal sitting at the counter? She's been smiling at me since I got here."

"Her name is Blanca," I said. Adding, that I didn't know anything about her.

"Well," he said, "I think I'll just go introduce myself." I cautioned Big Sal, warning him that I had reservations about Blanca; she could bring him trouble. He ignored me and joined her at the counter. I watched curiously, wondering if Blanca would turn him away. She smiled at Big Sal.

A few minutes later Big Sal ordered a beer for Blanca, which surprised me since up to now she'd only had Diet Cokes. Reaching into his pocket, he produced a thick wad of cash that he always carried with him. No doubt he wanted to impress Blanca. From then on, she fawned over him, laughing at his stale jokes which I'd heard before. Big Sal seemed captivated by Blanca's good looks and charm. They acted like newlyweds in love.

By midnight nearly everyone had cleared out. I told Big Sal I needed to close-up, since I had to open the cafe early the next morning. He promised to leave after Blanca returned from the restroom. With her gone, I got a chance to talk to him alone. I was worried.

"This isn't any of my business, but I think you'd better be careful with Blanca," I said.

Big Sal laughed and told me not to worry. "That pretty little thing couldn't hurt me." He'd played football in high school and, according to the local newspaper, he was one of the toughest linemen in the school's history.

"Just the same, you'd better be careful," I said. Afterwards he and Blanca drove off in his pickup truck.

The following morning Big Sal and a policeman were waiting for me in the cafe parking lot. I noticed that Big Sal was wearing the same clothes from the night before. He looked angry. "She robbed me," he cried out loud. "Can you believe it?"

Apparently, Blanca and Big Sal had gone to a nearby motel. When he woke up the next morning his wallet and money were gone. She'd even stolen his gold watch, an heirloom that had been in the family for generations. The policeman asked me what I knew about Blanca. I said she was a new customer. She didn't say much about herself. After a few more questions, the officer said hustlers like Blanca were cunning. "We'll do our best to catch her, but most likely she's already left town," he said. He promised to contact us if, by chance, they found her.

When the police left I pulled Big Sal aside. "Didn't I warn you about her?" "You're lucky she didn't slit your throat." Big Sal looked humiliated.

"She must have put something in my drink. All I remember is waking up alone and my wallet missing," said Big Sal, no longer his brash and arrogant self. "One last thing," he said, "please don't tell anyone about what happened. It's nobody's business." He said that if his wife found out, she'd divorce him for sure. I promised not to say a word. I'd never seen Big Sal so distressed.

A year later Blanca returned to the cafe. At first, I didn't recognize her. She'd lightened her hair and wore high heels that made her appear taller. Her unmistakable beauty, however, left no doubt who she was.

Blanca wasn't alone. She was with Gil Hernández and his son, Henry. They'd been steady customers for years. Gil owned property all over town, and even had a street named after him. He was one of the wealthiest businessmen in Riverside.

Gil wanted me to meet Blanca. "Memo, this is Henry's girlfriend, Blanca." He said that the couple had recently met, and he wanted to treat her to the best Mexican food in town. Blanca turned sheet-white as I reached out to shake her hand.

"Glad to meet you," I said, pretending to not recognize her. Blanca did likewise. She chatted about the cafe's quaintness, and how her family once owned a small cafe in Madrid.

"The food smells wonderful. I can't wait to eat," she said. What a liar, I thought. Poor Henry, he had no idea what he was up against.

The three of them sat at a table. I handed each of them a menu. "No need for that. Bring us three orders of chicken enchiladas and three iced teas," Gil said, not giving the couple a chance to read the menu. "The enchiladas here are outstanding. You'll love them," he told the couple. Henry nodded in agreement.

Moments later Henry was kneeling on the floor. As I got closer, I realized he was proposing to Blanca. She looked spellbound and unable to talk. After all, they'd just met a few days earlier. I heard Blanca say, "Yes." Henry then reached into his shirt pocket and pulled out a ring, which he carefully slipped onto her finger. I didn't know much about diamonds, but it looked expensive. Blanca gazed in my direction, and with her eyes pleaded with me not reveal her secret. That was the furthest thing from my mind.

Overcome with emotion, Gil embraced the couple. Then he stood and raised his glass of iced tea into the air. "Ladies and gentlemen. Can I please have your attention," he said to the few customers in the cafe. "I want to make a toast. My son Henry has just proposed to this lovely young lady, and she said yes. Please join me in toasting to their happiness; to Henry and Blanca!" Customers applauded. Gil thanked everyone, and then the three of them sat down to eat.

Blanca looked nervous, and I marveled how she handled the immense strain. After all, nothing prevented me from calling the police, or alerting Gil that his son's fiancée was a wanted fugitive. However, that would have been a mistake. It was obvious that Henry adored his Blanca, and nothing I said was going to change that. I'd keep our secret hidden in the basement of my mind. After finishing their meal, the happy couple said their final goodbyes and rushed off.

Gil seemed eager to talk afterwards. He moved his chair closer to mine. "That Blanca is really something special, and Henry is lucky to get her," he said.

"What do you know about her?" I asked, sounding inquisitive. After all, I remarked, I'd never seen her before. Was she from Riverside?

"She's not from around here. Her family is from Spain. Pure Spanish blood runs through her veins," boasted the proud soon-to-be father-in-law. I mentioned that Blanca looked Mexican, like the light-colored ones in the TV novellas. "Oh no, there's nothing Mexican about her. Blanca can trace her lineage to Spanish monarchs," protested Gil. "She's got real class."

"Henry picked out a great gal," I said. "I'm sure she will make him happy."

"She's definitely a winner. Anyone can see that," Gil said. He admitted Henry had acted in haste — impulsive. Something he'd never do. But he realized Henry was now a grown man, and had to make his own decisions. Gil said he could now die in peace knowing that his Henry had found true love.

The Jukebox Bandit

Jamie didn't look like a thief. He had a boyish face and seemed as trustworthy as an altar boy — incapable of stealing the cafe's beloved jukebox, which for years had entertained customers. On this day he was at the cafe picking up a food order and caught my attention when I saw him standing in front of the jukebox.

"Wait! Don't put in any money. It doesn't work," I shouted, thinking he was going to put a quarter in the coin slot.

"I wasn't going to," Jamie responded. He said he'd seen the "Out Of Order" sign and asked, "What's wrong with the jukebox?"

"I'm not sure. It just stopped playing," I said.

"It probably just needs a new fuse. Shouldn't be too hard to fix," Jamie said. "Do you mind if I take a look at it?"

I was skeptical. "Do you know anything about jukeboxes?" I asked.

"I know a lot about jukeboxes," Jamie said with unabashed confidence. "Growing up, I worked at my father's repair shop. We fixed everything — even jukeboxes." I gave my approval. Luckily, the jukebox's lock was broken, so he easily opened it up. After a quick inspection he said the machine was in good shape but needed new fuses and needed to be cleaned and oil.

"Would you be able to fix it today?" I asked.

"I'm booked solid today. But tomorrow I can be here bright and early," Jamie replied. He had good news. Our jukebox was a Seeburg, a well-known brand so parts wouldn't be hard to find.

"That's good news," I said. I told Jamie that the cafe had lost its vitality since the jukebox stopped working, and I was anxious to hear it play again. Jamie promised it wouldn't take long to fix. The jukebox had sentimental value. Over the years my father had loaded it with jazz, salsa, and boleros — music that he loved. At Tia Olga's insistence, country music was later added. Customers requested music that had a wider appeal, besides being more profitable, but Oscar flatly refused. He didn't care if the jukebox made money or not.

The next morning Jamie showed up toting a bulky toolbox. Within minutes he dismantled the jukebox, leaving a mishmash of small electronic components scattered on the counter. I thought of Humpty-Dumpty, the nursery rhyme character who fell and couldn't be put back together again. Seeing the jukeboxes' innards strewn about rattled me, so every chance I got I checked on Jamie. I asked how things were going.

He must have sensed my apprehension. To ease my fears, the young technician meticulously explained every part's function. I was impressed by his knowledge of circuits and transistors, which I knew nothing about. Confident that the jukebox was in good hands, I left him alone to finish. In fact, I'd forgotten he was there and turned my attention to other matters.

Minutes later the cafe's resident gamblers arrived. Made up mostly of elderly retired men, they spent their days wagering on thoroughbreds. Each had a copy of the Daily Racing Form, which printed detailed information on thoroughbreds racing that day. In jest, I'd dubbed them the Long Shots because they liked to bet on unlikely winners. It made sense. Horses who beat the odds paid off handsomely.

Like Wall Street traders, the Long Shots swapped insider information that circulated like salacious gossip. For instance, a visit by a veterinarian indicated a potential a leg injury, which could affect a horse's performance. In the past few months, I'd been learning to play the horses, and by sheer luck had picked a few winners. Some said I was a natural like my father, who kept files on thousands of horses.

One of the Long Shots, Marcus, had taken me under his wing. "Memo, who do you like in the fifth?" Marcus asked. The retired laborer moved to Riverside in the 1950s. He was from Georgia, and had left the state for good after a white mob tried to lynch his best friend. "I'm through with Georgia. You couldn't pay me to live there," he once told me.

"I like Little Leo in the fifth. That's my horoscope sign," I said. I didn't know anything about the horse, but I had a hunch he'd win. If he did, he'd pay off big since the odds of winning were against him.

"Maybe you got something there," Marcus said. He thought for a moment, and then remembered that this particular horse did well on muddy tracks. "With all the recent rains, he might win." Marcus had a knack for picking winners, and his opinion carried weight among the Long Shots. A few years earlier he'd won the 5-10 at Agua Caliente in Tijuana, Mexico: he'd picked six winners in a row, and won enough to buy a small house. His recall and analysis were remarkable for someone who'd dropped out of school in the third grade.

Travis interrupted. "Man don't listen to that crap. That horse is a loser. He hasn't won a race in years." Travis also belonged to the Long Shots, and often belittled his colleagues who he said didn't know anything. He claimed to have a reliable source at the racetrack who, for a nominal fee, supplied him with confidential information about horses and jockeys. Annoyed by the intrusion, Marcus told me to stick to my gut instincts and to ignore Travis. He said Travis was a loudmouth, and that his so-called informant was useless since Travis hadn't picked a winner in over a year.

The atmosphere inside the cafe changed when Brother B arrived. The local bookie operated out of a house on Park Avenue, but he often collected bets at the cafe. Oddly, he had no fear of the police, even taking bets in the dining room, in plain view of uniformed cops. They simply turned a blind eye. Rumor had it that Brother B bribed the police, but that was unlikely. He despised law all enforcement, who he said were merely thugs with badges. Once I saw him spit on a police cruiser parked in front of the cafe.

"Good morning, gentleman," said Brother B. He seemed to be in a hurry. "I don't have time for bullshit today. Once I'm out that door it's too late." Like a porter collecting fares on a crowded train, Brother B took cash from the Long Shots. Incredibly, he didn't use pen or paper and recorded every bet in his head. After twenty-five years in the book-making business, I heard him once crow, he'd never had a lapse in memory.

Marcus still hadn't placed his bet. "Man, I'm not too sure about that horse of mine." He'd been extra cautious lately and had a good reason to be. Even though he had a good pension, he was always broke and constantly borrowed money from friends. After his divorce, he sold his house and moved to a trailer park to cut down on expenses but still fell behind in his bills every month. I often didn't charge him for meals at the cafe.

"Why don't you bet on Little Leo? Didn't you say he runs well in the rain?" I reminded Marcus.

"Hey, that's right!" he said. "How could I be so dumb? Sure, he loves muddy tracks! Besides, he's overdue for a win." With renewed confidence, Marcus hurriedly placed his bet with Brother B, who minutes later left the cafe with a fistful of cash. With no more business to conduct, Marcus and the other Long Shots also left. It was then I noticed that the jukebox was gone and so was Jamie.

"Where's Jamie?" I asked Tia Olga, who'd been busy serving customers. She shrugged her shoulders.

"He left a while ago," she said. "Didn't you notice when he wheeled-out the jukebox? He passed right by you."

"Did he leave his phone number, or business card?"

"Jamie said you already had his phone number, and that he'd call you later today," Tia Olga replied. It occurred to me that he hadn't given me his phone number or business card. I had no way of contacting him. Tia Olga remembered that Jamie had a patch on his shirt pocket that read Apex Electronics. I looked in the phone book, but no such company existed. Tia Olga said I should call the police. However, without a name or phone number, that would be pointless.

Due to my carelessness, a sneaky thief had stolen the cafe's jukebox. I should have been more careful and not allowed myself to be distracted by foolish pastimes. Unable to afford a new one, we leased a jukebox from a rental business that stocked it with current Top Ten hits, which my father disliked — he never played it again. Instead of Duke Ellington, the Beatles now ruled the jukebox. To make matters worse, on the same day the jukebox was stolen, Little Leo came in last place.

Sarge

Everyone at the cafe knew him as Sarge. The WWII veteran, a sergeant in the U.S. Army, never passed an opportunity to entertain customers with his war stories. If true, his tall tales would have made him the most decorated soldier in history — even more heroic than Sergeant York, the celebrated soldier of WWI. Tragically, however, his glory days at the cafe ended when a small insect landed in his plate.

I stood at attention when Sarge entered the cafe. He saluted me with a quick snap, and then said, "At ease soldier." I relaxed. Sarge always livened up whenever I pretended to be a soldier. He said it reminded him of his army days. In fact, even after the war, he continued to wear his military issued dog tags. Even his license plate frame read, "Proud To Be A World War Two Veteran."

Margarita, the cafe's newest waitress, was on the phone so I took Sarge's order. "What will it be today, Sarge?"

He looked exhausted. "I'm dead tired and sure could use a cold beer." Sarge owned a small orange grove, which kept him busy. Now middle aged, the arduous work left him wearier than ever, and he drank to numb the shooting pain caused by a slipped disc. He said that his doctor wanted to cut into his spine, but the surgery was too risky — he decided to learn to live with the pain instead.

"One cold beer coming up," I said. Although just shy one year of twenty-one and not of legal age, I'd been allowed to pour beer since I could reach the tap handles. In fact, I had a flair for pouring beer, and I always left the right amount of foam.

Sarge drank like a sinkhole. "Fill her up again. On the double," he hollered, as I scrambled to refill his glass. He belched loudly after each swig. "Pardon me, but that couldn't be helped," he apologized. "I guess I drank too fast." I told him not to worry. Except for Margarita, we were alone.

After getting off the phone, I noticed that Margarita snarled when she saw Sarge. They'd quarreled in the past. "What will it be today?" she asked.

The old veteran grumbled. "I'm tired of eating the same old thing. I want something different," he said. Margarita handed him the menu, but he quickly pushed it aside. She suggested a recent addition called steak picado, which consisted of thin pieces of steak that came with onions and bell peppers. "Hey, that sounds really good. I'll take that," he said, "but hold my order until I've had a few more beers." He said he wanted to relax first.

In the meantime, Margarita got busy cleaning the beer cooler. She bent over to be able to reach inside, and that's when I noticed Sarge staring at her behind, even leaning over the counter to get a better look. "Hey Margarita, you sure have a nice caboose," he snickered.

Margarita straightened up and faced him. "I don't appreciate that kind of talk. This isn't a bar, and I'm not one of those barmaids who puts up with nonsense," she sternly replied.

"There's no need to get so angry," Sarge shot back. He went on to say that a waitress shouldn't be offended by a harmless compliment — after all, it was just part of the job. Moreover, Sarge quipped, God wired men to stare at big butts. "It's not our fault."

"Behave yourself. Remember what happened last time," Margarita warned. It wasn't her first tussle with the obnoxious veteran. Not long ago, she'd hit him with a wet towel after he tried to grope her. The blow left an ugly bruise on his face, which lasted several days. Apparently, Margarita wasn't a woman to be trifled with. She finished cleaning the cooler, and afterwards Sarge didn't bother her again.

Sarge's troubles worsened when Brett, a student at UC Riverside, arrived to pick up a food order. In the 1970s many students lived in the barrio to take advantage of low rents. I noticed that Brett seemed edgy. "Hey Memo. Is my food ready?" Brett asked. Usually, Brett was friendly and never in a hurry.

"In a second," I said, working as fast as I could. I tightly wrapped the tacos in foil and put them in a paper bag. "Finished at last." It was then that I discovered why Brett had been so nervous. All this time, Sarge had been glaring at him. Brett couldn't stand it any longer.

"Something on your mind, old man?" Brett said.

"You should be horsewhipped for wearing that shirt. It's disrespectful to our troops," Sarge said, referring to Brett's t-shirt that read, "Make Love Not War." At this time the Vietnam War had already ended, but the memory of students marching in the streets against the war was still fresh. "Because of people like you, too chicken to fight, we lost the war."

"Fuck you, old man," Brett angrily replied. "You don't know anything about me. In fact, I did three tours in Nam. I got shot in the chest and nearly bled to death." He offered to take off his shirt to show his scar but then changed his mind.

"That's a damned lie. The army wouldn't take a long-haired coward like you," Sarge cried out. He then hurled a beer bottle at Brett, which missed him and landed on the floor behind the counter. Remarkably Brett didn't fight back: apparently stunned by Sarge's brazen behavior. I was relieved. Much younger and stronger, he could have seriously injured the elder veteran. Seconds later Brett bolted.

Soon after I heard Brett knocking at the back door. He'd forgotten his food, but more importantly he said he wanted to apologize for the disturbance. I told him he wasn't to blame; it was Sarge's fault. I quickly handed him his order and told him he had to leave. Sarge, I said, made regular trips to the restroom and might find us here. Brett said he didn't want any more trouble and hurried out with his bag of tacos.

I returned to the dining room. Sarge, still upset, said I shouldn't let Brett back in the cafe. I answered that Brett was a good customer and welcome here. Sarge said people like Brett were traitors, and an insult to veterans like him who'd suffered during the war. He reminded me that he'd been a prisoner of war, and that he'd eaten insects to stay alive. I'd heard this story a million times and grown tired of it.

Thankfully, Sarge's food was done. This would calm him down, I thought. "How's the steak picado?" I asked.

"Wow, this is amazing," Sarge said. I told him that we'd marinated the meat, letting the seasonings soak in. Sarge said that he'd order it again.

I stepped outside for a moment. After a while, I went back inside and found Sarge sorting through his food. Maybe his wedding ring had slipped off and fallen in his plate. "Is there anything wrong, Sarge?" I asked.

"I think there's a bug in the steak picado," he said. He put on his reading glasses to get a closer look. Mixed in with the thin pieces of steak was the severed body of a large cockroach, the same kind I'd seen coming out of the sewer cleanout behind the cafe. Apparently, Sarge had cut the insect in half and inadvertently eaten its head.

I was mortified. "I'm so sorry, Sarge. Are you okay?" He'd turn pale and seemed disorientated — unable to talk. I worried that he might have a panic attack or worse. I tried to keep him calm. Then Sarge regained his composure. His color returned, along with his tough guy temperament. He was okay.

"Oh, don't fuss. It was just a harmless little bug," he said. "I'll be fine. In fact," he said in jest, "bring back that little critter and I'll eat whatever is left of him." I pretended to laugh, yet I wasn't amused.

Sarge told me not to worry. Reminding me, once again, that he'd developed a cast iron stomach during the war, and that he could eat almost anything and not get sick. Despite Sarge's insistence that he was fine, I wanted to compensate him for his troubles.

"Tonight, everything is on the house," I said.

"You don't have to do that. Don't be silly," he said.

"Put away your money — I insist." I tore up his bill and threw it in the trash. I told him he could order something else: free of charge. Sarge said he'd lost his appetite. Instead, he opened the newspaper to finish a crossword puzzle he'd started earlier. I returned to my kitchen duties at the rear of the cafe, out of sight of the dining room. Not long after, Margarita yelled out, "Come quick, it's Sarge."

I found Sarge slumped over on the counter. He'd vomited, and his body began to twitch as if he'd swallowed a minor earthquake. He collapsed on the floor and I immediately called the fire department. I stood by helplessly, not know-ing what to do. Margarita raised his head off the floor, and with a wet towel tenderly wiped Sarge's face. He stopped trembling, but still looked dazed and confused.

When the paramedics arrived, Sarge was still lying on the floor. He could barely talk. The paramedics checked his blood pressure, and then hooked him up to a monitor to check his heart. "Sarge wasn't in any immediate danger," said one of the paramedics. Adding, that he'd suffered a panic attack, which resembled a heart attack. Both paramedics recommended that Sarge go to the hospital. But he stubbornly refused, insisting nothing was wrong. Afterwards the medics packed up their gear and left.

Sarge apologized for the mess, and even offered to help clean. I told him that wasn't necessary. He didn't look well, so I offered to drive him home. He thanked me but said he could get there on his own. Before leaving, he thanked Margarita and even tried to give her a tip but she flatly refused. As he headed out the door, I didn't salute and neither did he; under the circumstances it didn't seem appropriate.

Apparently, the thought of a cockroach inside of him had made Sarge violently sick. If this was true, then his prisoner of war story was a lie. After all, hadn't he said he'd eaten insects to stay alive while in a Japanese prison camp? Margarita said Sarge was a phony, she'd known it all along. Moreover, she said she wouldn't miss him. He'd been disrespectful to her and awful to Brett — an incorrigibly, obnoxious man, she exclaimed. At the same time, she admitted that she felt sorry for him. His lies had come out of hiding and humiliated him in a cruel manner that no one deserved. I agreed.

Sitting at the counter (on the far-right) is John, the cafe's only white male employee. The other two persons are unknown customers.   circa 1964

Suzie Medina at the cafe after her First Communion. circa late 1960s

Collage of images from the first restaurant

Standing from left to right is Jon, Bill, Max and
Richard Rodela (our cousin and Tia Olga's son).

Max and Josefina sitting at the counter.   circa 1971

Rosa Bribiesca, Suzie Medina, Olga Rodela at the cafe.   circa 1974

Sitting at the far right of the photo is Uncle Leo Castro, and sitting directly across him is Tia Olga. The two male customers are unknown. circa 1978

Staff photo by Jim Edward

he family' at Zacatecas includes, standing clockwise from John edina (wearing glasses), Oscar Medina, Lucy Castro, Irma Me-

dina, Martha Mungia and Olga Rodela. Owner Oscar Medin leaves most of the cooking to the others.

Press Enterprise article about the cafe. circa 1983

Suzie Medina with Leer Larkin, who became a co-parent to the Medina children until his death in 1992. An artist himself, he ran an art workshop and gallery (Nosotros Fine Arts Workshop) in the shopping center a few doors from the cafe.   November 22, 1990.

Garden unlikely battle ground for culture, age

▶ His father owns a parking lot and plants corn there, claiming right to grow whatever pleases him. But the city has challenged sovereignty over the soil.

William O. Medina

Gardens usually evoke images of peace and serenity. They are treats to our vision. In the Spring when plants are blooming, and allay orbital blood pressure without ingesting pills. Yet our garden has become a hot spot, where cultural and generational battle lines have been drawn. The combatants are my father, city government, and myself.

Our garden isn't in a backyard, or in rural area hidden from view. Actually, our garden is the landscaping of a parking lot where customers park in front of our restaurant. And because it's semi-public, the issue of control has arisen. My father, who owns the parking lot and cares for it, claims the right to grow whatever pleases him. Yet the city has challenged dad's sovereignty, insisting that it has the final authority about what lives or dies on his soil.

I'm a pacifist, and always try to manufacture solutions whenever possible. En-mily serves no purpose, except to sour the stomach. Thus I tried to convince dad that fighting city hall was a losing proposition. He wanted to grow corn, squash and tomatoes. The city wanted attractive plants that are appropriate for a parking lot — both sides were prepared for trench warfare.

Unfortunately, dad wasn't in the mood for compromise last Spring when revisions were made to the parking lot. With the help of a friend, he planted corn and other needs against my protestations. After several weeks, dad's plants broke through the soil and inundated the parking lot with melons, squash, tomatoes and corn. It looked as though we'd ceased being a restaurant and became a fruit stand.

Tensions escalated in July when the corn was ready to be harvested. I thought dad's plants might provoke retaliation from the city since the corn could now be seen from the street. Corn wasn't on the landscaping plans and unsuitable for a parking lot, I reminded dad. A swift resolution was now light years away. Once his garden had taken root, compromise was unlikely — dad would never agree to uprooting his corn, which he says is the foundation of our people. It would be an attack on everything Mexican.

Dad likes to park his wheelchair close to his garden, and relished the praise from customers who stop to gaze at his plants. "Please, take whatever you like," dad often says. One afternoon, dad and his friend were in the parking lot roasting corn on his portable grill. I was shocked when I saw our customers eating corn — free of charge — with dad under a tree. Dad's garden was cutting into the cafe's profits!

In our culture, respect for elders is crucial. Thus an open challenge to dad's authority wasn't an option. Instead, I enlisted the incendiary tools of diplomacy. I needed a pretext to declare a moratorium on planting corn in the parking lot. It had arrived when people began to steal the corn and squash during the night. I provided dad a detailed account of what had been stolen, and expected him to become alarmed. Instead of reacting angrily, dad smiled. It pleased him to know that he was helping augment someone's dinner table, he explained. My strategy had failed.

My staunchest ally against dad was nature. In July we cut down the corn stalks, which were carted off by a man who used them to feed his cows. The watermelon had produced a sugarless interior and disappointed dad. And though the squash kept producing, the nocturnal garden looter couldn't be stopped. When winter arrived, my dad said it was time for the soil to sleep — the planters were stripped of everything green. It was during the winter cold months that I implemented Operation Reclaim.

With the assistance of Rusty, a local landscaper, we began planting palm trees without dad's knowledge. The cold is menacing to dad's delicate health, so he seldom ventures outside during winter. Within a few days, the parking lot was covered with Red Apple ground cover, Queen Palms and other typical parking lot plants. In his small truck, Rusty hauled tons of river rock to simulate a small creek between two palms. One day in January, when the sun flexed its muscle, dad came outside. When he saw that his garden was now occupied by invaders, he just smiled. "I've always liked palm trees," he said.

It's Spring, and until now dad hasn't violated our unwritten truce. We've been adding, with dad's approval, colorful plants within the concrete planters. However, I'm nervous, since it's that time of year when dad usually plants his corn. So far, though, dad hasn't asked for his corn seeds.

LOCAL VIEW

■ William O. Medina of Moreno Valley is an owner of Zacatecas Cafe in Riverside.

Column written by Bill Medina that appeared in the local newspaper. Oscar always had a garden, even while growing up in Riverside's Eastside neighborhood. In 1999 a code enforcement officer informed Oscar that "private gardens" were not allowed on commercial property. To appease code enforcement officials, he agreed to the planting of ground cover and palm trees. Press Enterprise. April 18, 1999.

SILVIA FLORES / THE PRESS-ENTERPRISE

Suzanna Medina Hernandez, right, receives a hug from Stella
Figueroa while celebrating with family, friends and patrons at
Zacatecas Cafe in Riverside.

Newspaper article on the cafe's 40th anniversary. Suzie, who is
in the photo, owned and managed the business at the time.
Press Enterprise. circa November 2003

Los Tres Hombres

One evening Mateo, whose house adjoined the cafe's back parking lot, stormed into the cafe. The teenager, filled with terror, had bruises all over his face. He said his father was after him and asked if he could hide inside the cafe. I told Mateo to go inside the restroom and to be quiet. And not to come out unless I said so. He'd be safe there.

After a few minutes, certain that his father wasn't outside waiting for him, I told Mateo to come out. "What happened?" I asked the frightened boy.

"It's my dad. He's trying to kill me," cried Mateo, who wore a Mickey Mouse t-shirt and a pair of old blue jeans. Although large for his size, he was just a boy who still went trick-or-treating on Halloween.

"Don't worry. No one is going to hurt you," I said. I showed him the baseball bat I kept under the counter and I promised to use it if his father stepped one foot inside the cafe. My brother Jon, who'd been listening, bolted the thick wooden door shut.

When he calmed down, Mateo told us that his father, Reyes Gomez, had threatened his mother and little sister tonight. He'd even smashed the telephone with a baseball bat. "That's why I ran inside the restaurant," Mateo cried out.

Curious, I asked, "What's made him so angry?"

"Crank calls. Someone keeps calling and hanging up — it drives him crazy," Mateo said, tears rolling down his face.

"Should I call the police?" I asked.

"What for, they won't do anything," Mateo said bitterly. He remarked that a few months ago Reyes had accused his mother of trying to poison him. He knocked out her front teeth. When the police arrived, they wouldn't arrest him. Instead, Mateo said, "The cops told us not to provoke him. As if it was our fault."

Mateo, still visibly upset, said he didn't want to talk about his father anymore. I didn't blame him. Jon and I got back to work. I finished washing the stack of dirty dishes. Meanwhile, Jon swept and mopped and cleaned the restroom. Within an hour we finished and got ready to leave. I asked Mateo if he had any relatives who'd let him spend the night. He lowered his head and answered no.

"You're welcome to stay with us," I said. Mateo seemed hesitant at first. After all, we barely knew him, but then he accepted. I told him that he needed to call his mother and let her know that he was staying with us. "She'll be worried."

"No! No! No! Calling will only irritate my father even more," Mateo insisted, his lips quivering with fear. "He might hurt my mother and sister." I remembered what he'd said earlier about the police not helping them and didn't mention it again. After I turned off the lights and locked the back door, the three of us left.

The cafe was only a few blocks from our house, so we arrived within minutes. Josefina, my mother, had never met Mateo before. "This is my friend Mateo," I said.

"It's so nice to meet you," Josefina smiled.

Mateo fidgeted from side to side. "Thank you," he said nervously.

"Can Mateo stay for a few days?" I asked. I told Josefina that his parents were painting his house, and the fumes were making Mateo dizzy. He'd even thrown up. I hated lying to Josefina, but I couldn't tell her the truth. She'd overreact and call the police, which Mateo didn't want.

"You can stay here as long as you want," Josefina said. Mateo didn't know it then, but he'd just checked into the equivalent of a five-star hotel. My mother, despite working long hours at the cafe, loved to cook for relatives and friends. Every Christmas our house teemed with guests, many of them customers who'd become close friends of the family. Even the cops came to eat. They stuffed themselves with tamales and her famous macaroni and cheese.

"I appreciate you letting me stay here," Mateo said.

"Are you boys hungry?" Josefina asked. I told her that I'd already eaten, but Mateo might want something to eat. Naturally shy, Mateo said he wasn't hungry. But I knew better. I'd heard his stomach grumbling in the car while on the way home.

"He's starving," I said.

Mateo's face turned red. "Don't be shy," Josefina said. "If your stomach is empty you've come to the right place." We followed her into the kitchen, overrun with pots and pans that she treated with care: much like a mechanic's affinity for tools. Josefina went straight to work. Jon didn't stay and instead went outside to check on our new dog, Goofy.

It didn't take long for Josefina to make a quesadilla, which Mateo quickly devoured. He asked if he could have another; his shyness apparently gone. My mother told him he could eat as much as he wanted. It turned out that Mateo had the appetite of ten football players, and he didn't stop eating until all the cheese and tortillas were gone. My mother looked worn out but never complained.

We didn't have an extra bedroom, so Mateo had to bunk with me and Jon. It was crowded but I didn't mind, even though by then I was an adult and needed my own space. With only two beds, Josefina set out a sleeping bag she'd bought at K-Mart for my cousin Ricky, who on occasion stayed with us. Even our dog Goofy, who didn't like strangers, immediately took to Mateo and often slept next to him on the floor. A week passed and Mateo still hadn't gone home.

In time Mateo adapted to our daily routine. In the evenings Mateo helped at the cafe. With an extra hand we finished early and had time to sit outside and watch the bustle on University Avenue. Most of the time, though, we just talked, mainly about girls or teachers we hated. I'd graduated, but the memories of high school were still fresh in my mind. Then one night, while sitting outside, Mateo unexpectedly opened up about his father's mental illness. Jon and I listened attentively.

Mateo said that for the past two years Reyes had made their lives unbearable — a living hell, as he described it. He recounted the night when, while asleep, he heard a clicking sound. He woke up and his father was standing over him holding a pistol. "I jumped out of bed and ran. Reyes chased me but I was too fast." Mateo said he didn't come home for five days after that. I asked him if he thought Reyes had been playing Russian roulette that night with him. He said yes.

"He's a psycho," Jon cried out, adding that Reyes belonged in Patton State Hospital along with the other crazies.

"He thinks assassins are out to get him," Mateo said, explaining that Reyes had become more and more paranoid in the past few months.

"Assassins! Who'd want to kill him?" Jon asked.

"I don't know. But he's convinced three men are trying to murder him. He calls them Los Tres Hombres. It's all in his head." Mateo said on the night he ran to the cafe someone had been calling and hanging up. Reyes said it was them.

"Try calling the police again. This time make them understand that your father is crazy and dangerous," I said. Mateo, distracted, had stopped listening to me. His eyes were suddenly fixed on his house. I also turned around. His backyard, brightly lit, looked like Dodger Stadium during a night game and emitted a sense of urgency and dread. Expecting trouble, Reyes had installed flood lights throughout the backyard.

"Something must be wrong," Mateo cried out. He stood on top of a chair to get a better look. "It looks like someone is in the backyard." The glare was blinding, which made it difficult to see clearly. "It's my dad. He's got a gun!" Mateo quickly ran into the cafe and called home, but no one answered.

"Mateo, call the police. Right now," I said.

He ignored my pleas, and said he needed to get home right away. "I want to make sure my mother and sister are safe," Mateo said. Jon and I followed him across the parking lot to his house. Reyes was on the front porch, and he had a gun. The three of us hid behind a large pepper tree and didn't make a sound. Then, as if he had psychic powers and could sense our presence, Reyes looked in our direction. He'd spotted us.

Without warning, he started shooting. Bullets struck the tree where we'd taken cover and pieces of bark rained down on us. We were under siege and had to get away from there, so the three of us ran as fast as we could. But Mateo didn't get very far. A bullet had struck his leg and he lay in the middle of the street, bleeding. I felt like a coward for not helping him, but that would have been suicide. Seconds later Reyes walked over to Mateo, took aim, and pulled the trigger. I heard a clicking sound but no gunfire — evidently, he'd run out of bullets. Oddly enough, Reyes bent over and muttered a few words to Mateo. I couldn't imagine what a father could say under the circumstances. Reyes then ran back inside the house.

The police arrived and surrounded the house. From the living room that faced the street, Reyes shouted obscenities and threatened to shoot anyone who got close. Neighbors gathered to watch the excitement. The standoff, however, didn't last very long. Despite his bravado, Reyes surrendered without a fight. Outfitted like commandos, the police must have terrified him. Mateo's mother and sister, luckily, had escaped through the back door and were safe.

The next day Jon and I visited Mateo in the hospital. Despite hospital rules prohibiting outside food, we sneaked in a burrito from the cafe. In minutes his room smelled like refried beans and chile verde. Surprisingly, the nurses didn't object. Mateo inhaled his burrito and asked if we'd brought another. Unfortunately, I said, we'd only brought one but promised to bring an extra one next time. For three hours, the three of us watched television and talked until a nurse said visiting hours were over. Before we left, Mateo thanked us for the burrito and for everything we'd done for him.

Strangely, Mateo stopped coming to the cafe after he got out of the hospital. On occasion I'd see him walking home from school, or in his backyard milling about. We'd talk now and then but only briefly. I'd invite him to the cafe for something to eat, but he always declined. I even tried visiting him at home, but his mother always said he was busy. Then one day he showed up at the cafe.

Mateo had good news. Reyes had pleaded guilty, so there'd be no trial. He'd be in prison for a long time, said Mateo who seemed relieved. In addition, he said they were moving to Arizona to live with his grandparents. They lived on a small farm outside of Tucson, and they had plenty of space and even had pigs and goats. I told Mateo that we'd miss him, but I understood why they had to leave. After a warmhearted embrace, we parted company. A week later Mateo was gone.

Plumbing Troubles

The nightmare started when a foul stench flooded the cafe. It hovered like thick summer smog, and forced diners to leave before they could finish eating. I opened all the doors and turned on the ceiling fans to clear out the awful stench. However, the odor wouldn't budge, so I closed the cafe.

Then Jon yelled out. "Memo, the sinks are all plugged up." I went to see for myself. "Look! The water won't go down," Jon said pointing to the putrid water. Even the toilet wouldn't flush. I told Jon not to worry, that I'd call Cano's Plumbing right away.

As usual, Cano didn't pick up his phone. Most likely he was probably under a house fixing a leaky pipe, so I left a message on his recorder. "It's Memo from the cafe. Come quickly," I hollered into Sally, the name he'd given his answering machine. He joked that Sally was the best secretary in the world. She worked for free and never needed a break.

Two hours later Cano's van pulled into the cafe's parking lot. Jon, who'd been keeping an eye out for him, called out, "He's here."

"What's the matter?" Cano asked as he trudged into the kitchen.

"All the drains are stopped up," I said.

"I bet the mainline is clogged again," Cano said. We walked outside to the cleanout, located behind the cafe. A puddle of black water had formed around the opening. It smelled awful.

"That's gross," said Jon, who went back inside and shut the door. The smell of sewage sickened him, which is why he flat out refused to clean the toilets at the cafe.

Unfazed, Cano told me not to worry. It was an easy fix, he assured me. He moved his van to the rear of the cafe and parked next to the cleanout. Inside was Cano's legendary drain cleaner, which he'd named El Chingon. "This machine is badass. It's never met a drain it couldn't open," Cano crowed.

"It looks heavy," I said. "Do you need a hand getting it off the van?" Cano laughed mockingly, and said he'd been unloading the brawny machine by himself for years. In no time El Chingon was on the ground. He turned it on and slowly shoved the cable into the drain.

"The cable is going in freely," I said. Cano remarked that the first few feet were always easy. The problem lay ahead. He was right. A moment later the cable abruptly stalled. "There's something in the pipe blocking the cable," Cano said, who didn't look surprised. He tried ramming the cable through, but without success. After a while he retracted the cable. "Come home to Papa," Cano said, who often spoke to his tools as if they were his children.

"What's wrong?" I asked. Cano showed me a fragment of crystalized grease that he'd fished out of the drain. He explained that over time grease accumulated and hardened, and it clogged drains. Much like a clogged artery, he said. His explanation didn't make sense to me, since I always thought of restaurant grease as soft and benign, incapable of creating so much mischief.

"Don't worry. I've got a secret weapon," Cano said. He went to his van and brought back a special tool called a cutter. "You see that son of a bitch, it eats concrete for breakfast." He attached the tool to the cable and then kissed it for good luck.

As before, the cable got only a few feet and then stopped. But this time Cano didn't give up so easily. The seasoned plumber used the cable like a battering ram. With all his might, he shoved the cable into the drain again and again. He breathed heavily. He wasn't young anymore, and at times he stopped to rest. Finally, his tenacity paid off. Cano had broken through.

"You did it!" I shouted with excitement.

Cano got on his knees and hugged El Chingon. "Gracias for not letting me down, hombre."

Jon, who'd been in the kitchen the entire time, ran outside with good news. "Hey, the water went down. Come and see for yourself." I went into the kitchen and found every sink bone dry — even the stench had vanished.

When I rejoined Cano outside, he was busy loading El Chingon into the van. "Can I get you a glass of water?" I asked.

"Hell no!" Cano said. "Bring me a beer instead, and make sure it's icy cold." He drank the beer and then three more. Cano boasted he could finish a case of beer in one night. I suspected he might be an alcoholic.

"I appreciate you coming out tonight," I said. Cano said he and my father were old friends; I could always count on him. I told him that my father was in the hospital. "He had a stroke, but it was a mild one," adding that my mother refused to leave his side. Until they returned, Jon and I were running the business.

"So sorry to hear that. Tell him I hope he gets well soon," Cano said. Right then his beeper went off. "It's Carlos Market. It's an emergency. I have to get there right away." Jon and I helped him gather his tools and then he left.

Our grease troubles didn't end that night. The next day a health inspector came calling. "Are you the owner of the cafe?" asked a man who introduced himself as Mr. Jones. Apparently, a neighbor had called to complain about the smell of raw sewage, and he'd been sent out to investigate.

"The business belongs to my parents, but they aren't here. My brother and I are in charge," I said. Mr. Jones, who wore a white uniform and shiny badge got right to the point.

"I found traces of fecal matter in the parking lot behind the cafe," Mr. Jones said. He explained that in such a case he had no alternative but to close the cafe until the problem was resolved.

"That won't be necessary," I replied. I told him that I'd already called a plumber, who came out that night and un-clogged the drains. "The problem has been fixed."

"I'd like to see for myself," Mr. Jones said. We went inside. He opened the faucet all the way and watched the water go down the drain — so fast that it made a slurping noise. I felt vindicated. Maybe he'd apologize for acting so hastily, I thought.

Instead, Mr. Jones looked under the sink. "Is there anything wrong?" I asked.

"Where's your grease trap?" inquired Mr. Jones.

"What's a grease trap?" I responded. I had no clue what he was talking about. I'd never seen one before.

"It's a small canister that's attached to the drain and pre-vents grease from getting into the main sewer line," he said. He added that the code had changed: all restaurants were now required to have large grease traps made of concrete that were in the ground. "I'm sorry, but the cafe must remain closed until you've met the new guidelines." After writing his report, Mr. Jones left.

I immediately called Cano, who was nearby and arrived within minutes.

"Let me see the report," Cano said, snatching the paper out of my hands. "Mr. Jones is dead wrong." He explained that the new rules didn't apply to older restaurants, so I had nothing to worry about.

"That's good news," I said.

"You're in the clear," Cano said, trying to cheer me up. He said that even if I had to install a new grease trap, the landlord would have to bear the cost. "You won't have to pay a cent." He apologized for not being able to stay longer but promised to return later. Meanwhile, he'd look into the cost of a new grease trap — just in case, he said.

I called Mr. Jones right away. I repeated what Cano had said about how the cafe was exempt. In a firm voice, Mr. Jones said the new law applied to all restaurants. He couldn't make an exception. I wanted to call my parents and give them the bad news, but Jon said they already had enough to worry about. We'd have to figure out how to fix the problem ourselves.

Early the next day I called Mr. Golden, our landlord. His secretary said he'd been trying to reach me all morning. She put me on hold while she connected me to his private line.

"What the hell is going on with my building?" Mr. Golden shouted. "The goddamned health department called.

They're going to fine me if I don't clean up the shit behind the cafe!"

"Mr. Golden, please calm down. It's not as bad as it sounds," I said. He quieted down. I told him about the clogged drains, and how raw sewage had leaked into the parking lot. However, the problem had been resolved, I explained. "Everything is fine now, except for one thing. The health department won't let me reopen unless I install a new grease trap."

"That's not my problem," Mr. Golden blurted out. He said that a new grease would be expensive, and he refused to pay. "I won't spend another penny on that old broken-down building," exclaimed Mr. Golden. It was true. Mr. Golden hadn't made any repairs to the cafe for some time. The roof leaked, and the old water heater leaked deadly fumes which I could smell in the winter when all the doors were closed.

I gently reminded him that under our lease agreement the landlord was responsible for major plumbing repairs.

"I don't care what the lease says! I'm not paying for a new grease trap," snapped Mr. Golden. I told him that I'd take him to court if he didn't live-up to the lease agreement. He laughed out loud and said, "Good luck with that," and then hung-up the phone. He was a partner in a big law firm in Los Angeles, and he'd devour us in court.

Upset, I called Cano right away. I told him what Mr. Jones had said about needing a new grease trap. And, that our landlord refused to pay for any of the costs. Unfortunately,

Cano had more unpleasant news. "A new grease trap will be mighty expensive," he said. Adding that with parts and labor it could cost around five thousand dollars.

"We don't have that kind of money!" I said. The kind-hearted plumber told me not to worry. He offered his labor free of charge. I thanked Cano, but pointed out that even if he donated his labor, we still didn't have enough money in the bank to cover the costs. "I guess we'll just have to find a way to raise enough cash."

Early the next day Cano arrived with terrific news. "Memo, your troubles are over!" He'd discovered a loophole in the building code that allowed small businesses, like ours, to install smaller grease traps. The best part, Cano said, was that they cost only a fraction of the larger models.

"Exactly how much less?" I asked.

"Around six-hundred dollars," Cano said. He'd brought a brochure with him which showed a diagram of the scaled down version. It consisted of a metal box no bigger than a large suitcase and a removable lid that provided access for daily cleaning. I'd have to clean it every night, warned Cano. "And the smell will be awfully bad."

"I don't care about the smell. I'll take it," I said. We shook hands, and then Cano left to make the arrangements for the installation.

Three days later Cano, along with two helpers, installed the grease trap, which he mounted outdoors behind the cafe.

When they finished, as a test run, Jon washed a few pots that had been sitting in the sink, all of them riddled with hardened grease. The new system worked perfectly. The next day I called the health department and requested a re-inspection.

I showed Mr. Jones the new grease trap. He gazed down at the contraption with disapproval. "I don't like these dwarf grease traps. They require daily maintenance, and almost always fail," Mr. Jones said. "I'll make weekly inspections for a year, and if I find excessive amounts of grease in the main sewer line, I'll have to close you down again." He said I could now reopen.

Months passed without any plumbing mishaps. And, just as he said, Mr. Jones inspected the grease trap each week. He admitted that at first, I seemed too immature to keep up with the daily cleaning. But I'd proved him wrong. The cafe passed every inspection with flying colors.

One day, as I was cleaning the grease trap, Cano unexpect-edly showed up. "You look a little pale, Memo. Are you okay?" Cano asked.

"I didn't realize grease could smell so bad," I said. "It re-minds me of rotten eggs." I told Cano that, by now, I should have gotten used to the foul odor, but instead I puked nearly every time I opened the lid.

"Ask Jon to help. The both of you could take turns," Cano suggested.

"Jon won't get near it. He can't stand the stink," I replied.

Cano went to his truck and returned with a jar of Vicks; an overpowering ointment used to relieve congestion. "Shove this up your nose. It blocks nasty smells. I use it all the time, especially when I'm knee deep in shit."

I did as he said but to no avail. By now the noxious fumes had seeped into my brain and no ointment, no matter how potent, was going to extinguish it. I even smelled it in my dreams. I told Cano that my father was now out of the hospital and that the stroke had left him partially paralyzed. He might retire. Cano said that it was now up to me to run the business. I agreed. Before he left, I gave Cano a warm embrace and thanked him for all that he'd done.

Although the new grease trap had saved the cafe, I nonetheless grew to detest it. The daily cleanings were becoming more and more unbearable. Eventually, I'd reach my breaking point and no longer be able to tolerate the oppressive stench. When that time came, the health department would surely shut down the cafe. Until then our family business lived on borrowed time.

Goodbye Old Cafe

They seemed to be everywhere, even in the wooden shelves in the kitchen. Left unchecked, termites would destroy the cafe and end our family business. It was time to call Roach Squad Exterminators, who quickly dispatched Glen Beck, their most experienced technician.

Glen arrived and went right to work. "You've got termites all right." Glen said, using his flashlight to illuminate the mounds of termite droppings under the sink. He removed sections of the wall under the sink which, over the years, due to moisture, had deteriorated. There, inside the wall, he found a burgeoning termite colony. He said termites like dark damp places. "It's paradise for them."

"How serious is the problem?" I asked.

"I won't know until I finish looking around," Glen said. I noticed that during his inspection he couldn't takes his eyes off the large cracks in the ceiling. "I need to get on the roof to take a look," he said with a sense of urgency. He went to his truck and returned with a ladder. Minutes later I heard him walking on the roof. With each step, loose plaster sprinkled down like light rain over the dining room. Before long he climbed down.

"Did you find any termites up there?" I asked.

He said that they had eaten through the rafters, weakening the entire roof structure. "It feels like a darn trampoline up there," he said. Adding, that the ceiling could collapse at any moment.

I felt a sense of dread. Jon had always had my back, but now he was working as an apprentice electrician and living in Los Angeles. I'd have to face the termite problem without him. And, although Oscar had recovered from his stroke, he was now semi-retired. Josefina, my stalwart mother, had become the cornerstone of the family business but she too was preoccupied, caring for my father. "Can the roof be fixed? I asked.

"Yes, but the repairs will be very expensive," Glen replied. He seemed anxious to get back to work. "I don't want to sound rude, but could you please leave me alone while I inspect the walls?" He needed privacy and complete silence.

"No problem. I'll just wait outside," I said. I stood near the backdoor, enjoying the cool evening air. Afterwards, I heard Glen talking to someone. I thought it odd, since I'd already closed for the day and he was alone inside.

He called out, "I know you're in there. You little devils can't hide from me."

Curious, I went into the kitchen and found Glen with his ear against the wall. I'd startled him. "Who are you talking to?" I asked.

"I'm talking to the termites," he said.

I laughed nervously. "Termites can't talk."

Josefina and Oscar Medina standing in front of the cafe (located on University Avenue and Park) on moving day. The landlord, unfortunately, had decided to tear down a section of the shopping center that included the cafe. The building was demolished a few days after this photo was taken.   circa May 1984

"But they do — at least to me they do," Glen said. He said he'd been talking to roaches and termites for years. "That's how I find them inside the walls." Glen said he wasn't crazy. After all, he pointed out, people talk to dogs, cats, and goldfish; no one thinks they're crazy. He had a valid point, so I dropped the subject.

"Did you find more termites in the walls?" I asked.

He didn't have encouraging news. "Every wall is heavily infested," he said. Glen had cut out an opening in the wall so I could see how the termites had bored through the wood studs. A termite flew by. "You see, there goes one now." "I'd noticed more of them lately — flying around," I said. Glen guessed that the termites had been in the walls for years; I just hadn't paid attention to them until now. They'd caused extensive damage, and he advised me to hire an engineer who could assess the structure before spending money on fumigation; he called it tenting. Before leaving, he handed me a copy of his report and wished me good luck.

Without my knowledge, Glen had sent a copy of the termite report to the city building department. Within a week a team of inspectors examined every inch of the cafe. They measured cracks in the walls and ceiling and collected termite droppings. One of the inspectors even climbed onto the roof, but immediately got down. I heard him say it was too dangerous up there. Their stern mannerism terrified me. When they finished, one of them posted a notice that declared the building unsafe.

Despite our best efforts we couldn't save the building. Even Mr. Golden, our landlord, who'd previously vowed not to spend another dime on the building, offered to make the needed repairs. However, the termites had eaten the cafe down to the bone, sounding its death knell. A final review by the city's engineering department sealed the cafe's fate: demolition. Three months later a wrecking crew brought down the old cafe.

Oscar, despite his ill health, wasn't ready to quit the restaurant business. Together with a Mr. Adams, a realtor, they'd found a new location for the cafe. My father called a family meeting. "I've got great news! I've found a new home for the cafe: the old Duke's Cantina." He said that although the former bar was rundown, with hard work it could be restored, adding, that Mr. Adams knows a contractor who works dirt cheap. My parents signed a lease agreement later that week and began construction. It turned out, however, that fixing up the old bar would be the least of our worries.

The new cafe was only two blocks from a church. Its pastor, who went by Pastor O, didn't waste time expressing his disapproval when he heard the cafe was moving into the old bar. Like Duke's Cantina, we served beer, and for him that was unacceptable. He didn't want alcohol anywhere near his church.

Pastor O had good reason to be worried. Duke's Cantina had been one of the rowdiest bars in town. For years he'd pressured the city to shut it down and, with the help of his congregants, even picketed the bar in the evenings. The watering hole, however, was popular among the locals and weathered Pastor O's attempts to put it out of business. Sadly, it took a brawl that escalated into a triple homicide for the police to finally close it for good. Years later, the family of the victims still left flowers behind the cafe in remembrance.

Pastor O, determined to prevent alcohol from cropping up near his church, had done his homework. Under the current law, which didn't apply to Duke's Cantina since it opened before the restrictions, alcohol sales near a church were prohibited. With the law on his side, Pastor O filed a complaint at city hall against the cafe. In a conciliatory letter to us, he regretted resorting to such harsh tactics and said that he had nothing against Mexican food, but only objected to the beer. Nevertheless, at our cafe, Mexican food and beer were inextricably linked. Without the foamy spirit, customers would go elsewhere.

I filed for an exemption at city hall, which would have allowed us to serve alcohol despite the church's proximity. But, in order to succeed, I needed to win over Pastor O. With his endorsement, I'd have a better chance of getting city approval.

At my request, I asked Pastor O if we could meet. He agreed but insisted that we meet at his church. "Please, come in and have a seat," he said. We shook hands. Although polite, he seemed resolute, and not in the mood for idle chatter. I got down to business.

"I understand your disapproval of alcohol, but our restaurant isn't Duke's Cantina," I said. I explained that we'd been in business for many years and had a solid reputation in the community. I told him the mayor was a regular customer, and that the *Los Angeles Times* had recently featured the cafe in its food section. However, in the past, the cafe had had its share of rowdy incidents.

He remained incredulous. "This is a house of worship. I've worked hard to build its membership and I must protect it," he insisted. He said the cafe, most likely, would be no different than the bar.

I reassured Pastor O that we posed no harm to his church. We did serve beer, I said, but it wasn't our main business. "We make our money mainly selling burritos, not beer," I said.

He replied that some church members were recovering alcoholics, so beer at a nearby business would be a big temptation. "I'm trying to help people stay sober," he said. In fact, he admitted, he'd been in recovery himself for five years from alcoholism and knew first-hand the struggle to stay sober.

"I disagree," I said, pointing out that many of his congregants were some of the cafe's most loyal customers and seemed indifferent to the beer at the adjoining tables. "I didn't see the harm." He still wouldn't relent. We parted with no solution in sight, but then a miracle happened — I realized then, that miracles had winners and losers.

Not long afterwards, I drove by Pastor O's church and saw him loading boxes into a moving truck. He flagged me down.

"As you can see we're moving," he said, sweat dripping down his face.

"Why?" I asked.

"Termites!" he exclaimed. They had devoured a massive load-bearing beam that supported the roof. "We've tented the building twice, but to no avail. The termites keep coming back." He lamented that the church, on the verge of

Josefina and Oscar at their new location which was on
University Avenue and Sedgwick.   October 1985

collapse, had been declared unsafe. Unable to afford the
necessary repairs, the city ordered it to be torn down.

I told Pastor O that I was sorry for his misfortune and
mentioned that we too had been victimized by termites in a
similar manner. "What will you do now?" I asked.

Strangely, he seemed optimistic. "Not to worry! God has
found us a new church," he said. "It's a mile from here and
the building is termite free." However, he added, his bad
luck was a blessing for the cafe. With his new church far

from the cafe, the alcohol restrictions no longer applied. I thanked him for not being resentful and promised him the cafe wouldn't be another Duke's Cantina. He looked at me and said, "I hope not," and then he left.

With the construction completed, we finally opened the new location. To celebrate, my parents held a lavish grand opening. There was standing room only. Even the mayor showed up and cut the obligatory ribbon. A hard driving mariachi played until midnight, and beer flowed freely but not enough to breach the promise I'd made to Pastor O. At Josefina's insistence, the local parish priest blessed the new building to protect it from harm. For me, though, his blessings weren't enough — I'd seen termites tear down a church. The next day, I hired Roach Squad Exterminators, who sent Glen to spray every inch of the building.

The Nopal Crisis

One morning Josefina sent me to get nopales (cactus paddles) for the cafe. She needed them right away to make the lunch special, so I ran as fast as I could. Within minutes I arrived at El Lote, a small vacant lot a few blocks from the cafe. Nopales grew there in abundance, enough for everyone in the neighborhood, including the cafe.

I went straight to work, cutting the nopal with a machete that Josefina kept in the kitchen. I worked fast, but careful not to let the unforgiving spines jab me too badly. Afterwards my back ached. I straightened up, and that's when I noticed a police car parked across the street. It hadn't been there before.

It was Red, a policeman who'd recently been assigned to our neighborhood. He was watching me; his presence made me feel uneasy since I wasn't doing anything wrong. Afterwards he drove off, so I continued to work.

Too busy, I hadn't noticed that Red had returned. "Freeze!" he said. "Slowly put the machete down." I looked up. Red had his hand on his gun and he walked towards me. Paralyzed by fear, I didn't comply right away. In a stern voice, he said, "I'm not going to tell you again, drop the machete." I complied.

Red patted me down, as he said, to make sure I didn't have weapons. "Why are you hassling me? I haven't broken any laws," I asked.

"You're taking property that doesn't belong to you. That's called stealing," Red replied.

I told him that people have been taking nopales from this empty lot for years. "Until now, the police have looked the other way," I said, adding that he was making a mistake.

Red was unconvinced. "Well, that doesn't change any-thing — stealing is stealing." Red handcuffed me and put me inside the patrol car, which he said was necessary for his safety. I'd never been detained by the police before, nor locked in a patrol car. I felt like a common criminal, even thought I'd done nothing wrong.

A small crowd had gathered. I heard someone say, "Look, he's got Oscar's son in the back seat." Red seemed nervous and kept a watchful eye on the on-lookers while he talked on the police radio. He had good reason to be vigilant. People in the neighborhood despised him. He was brash and aggressive. And he routinely pulled over people for no reason. Recently, while on patrol, someone had thrown a rock at his cruiser.

Moments later the crackling noise of the radio stopped; the dispatcher said I had no warrants. After letting me out of the police car, he took off the handcuffs, which had left a bruise on my wrists. I asked, "Can I go now?"

He blocked my path. "I'm not done with you yet." Red said he was letting me go with a warning. He explained that tak-ing plants without the owner's permission was illegal. From now on, he cautioned, he'd arrest anyone who took nopales from the empty lot. Red asked if I had any questions. I said no, and then he got into his police car and drove off.

Except for a wino affectionately known as T-Bird, the crowd had dispersed. He got that name because he only drank Thunderbird wine, the preferred alcoholic drink among the local winos. He asked me what was going on. I told him that Red had tried to arrest me for taking nopales from El Lote. "What! Everybody takes nopales from here," T-Bird said. "Don't listen to him. That cop doesn't know what he's talking about." I asked T-Bird if he knew who owned the vacant lot. "Who knows? I've lived in this neighborhood my entire life, and I've never met or seen the owner. The only people I see there are the kids who use it to play baseball." T-Bird asked me if I could spare a few cents. I gave him a quarter and I returned to the cafe — empty handed.

"Memo, where's the nopales?" Josefina asked. I tried to explain what had happened, but she abruptly cut me off, saying she didn't have time to hear excuses.

As the lunch hour approached the cafe began to stir with customers. Most patrons were regulars, including Fr. Silva, the priest at St Mary's. I offered him a menu, which he politely declined. "I Don't need it. I know exactly what I want. Bring me an order of nopales."

"I'm sorry father, but we don't have nopales today," I said. I told Fr. Silva that he'd have to order something else.

"Oh no!" said the disappointed priest. He went on about how he'd been craving nopales all morning.

Father Silva deserved an explanation. I told him that Red had tried to arrest me when I went to El Lote to get nopales, a property he was familiar with since it wasn't far from the church. "That's why there aren't any," I said. Adding, that Red had handcuffed me and even detained me inside his police car. I told Fr. Silva that Red threatened to arrest anyone he caught taking nopales from El Lote without permission."

He said that people in the community had been complaining about the overzealous cop. He even gave Mrs. Ortega, the church's choir director, a ticket for jaywalking. "How outrageous!" Before leaving, Fr. Silva promised to call the mayor to see what could be done. "We'll straighten this out, I promised."

Nopales ranked high in popularity at the cafe. In the 1970s, The *New Yorker Magazine* had featured an article that mentioned the cafe's nopales. People came as far away as Santa Barbara for the cactus dish. Disappointed customers complained. One man in particular, Major Harry Wilt, exploded when he heard the bad news. He'd driven all the way from Palm Springs. He couldn't understand how the cafe could run out of nopales since they seemed to grow everywhere. In fact, the alley behind the cafe teemed with nopales, but they were old and tasteless. "What's the problem? Just go get more!" Major Wilt said, pounding his fist on the counter.

"It's not that simple," I said. I couldn't tell him what had happened. Major Wilt struck me as a law-and-order Republican, and I doubted that he'd take sides against an abusive cop. Instead, I told him that we'd used up our supply of nopales. All we could do was wait for another delivery. Flustered, Major Wilt got in his car and left.

Later that afternoon Fr. Silva returned. He seemed anxious and said he needed to talk to me right away. "I have an idea that might work!"

"What do you have in mind?" I asked, encouraged by his optimism.

"Let's contact the property owner and request a letter in which he gives the entire neighborhood permission to take nopales from El Lote," Fr. Silva said. It would stop the harassment from the police. His plan was worth a try, but first we needed to find who owned El Lote, and then get a mailing address.

The next day Fr. Silva and I combed the neighborhood. We went door to door, asking people if they knew who owned El Lote. We got nowhere. It seemed odd that a parcel of land, so well-known in the community, could exist in anonymity. People had been gathering nopales from El Lote for generations. Fr. Silva remained undeterred. He said our next move was to visit the County Hall of Records, where we'd surely find the mysterious property owner.

Luckily, we found a sympathetic clerk named Ruben who worked in the records department. It turned out that he once lived on 10ᵗʰ Street, which was near the cafe. And, coincidentally, he'd been baptized at St. Mary's. Fr. Silva explained our dilemma, stressing that we needed a mailing address to contact the current property owner right away.

Ruben unraveled a map of the neighborhood, which clearly showed El Lote. "That's it. Right there," I said, putting my finger on the map where the nopales grew wildly.

"Hey! I know that property," Ruben exclaimed. "My mom used to send me there to get nopales, especially during Lent when meat wasn't allowed on Fridays." Adding, that he used to play baseball on the empty lot, and that he once hit a line drive that broke a window. "We all ran as fast as we could before the owner came out."

"Can you find out who owns the property? We tried on our own but got nowhere," Fr. Silva said.

"Sure," Ruben said. He promptly typed El Lote's address into the computer. Within seconds the name Calvin Berry appeared on the screen and with it a mailing address. "Got it!" Ruben blurted out.

Just as Fr. Silva had suspected the owner didn't live in the area. "That's why no one has ever seen him!" Fr. Silva said. He hurriedly wrote down the information and stuck it in his pocket. "Now that we have his address, we can write him." Before leaving, Fr. Silva gave Ruben a blessing and promised to keep him informed.

Rather than return to the cafe, Fr. Silva and I went straight to his office to write Mr. Berry. I'd never been inside the church rectory and felt privileged to be invited. However, to my surprise, his office lacked style. It was small, windowless and cluttered with stacks and stacks of papers. For someone so close to God I expected more — maybe a vintage oak desk or a plush leather chair. On his desk sat an old manual typewriter, which appeared broken and forgotten.

"Why don't you use an electric typewriter?" I asked. Fr. Silva laughed and said that the newer machines were too fast and complicated. He preferred the older models, which were better suited to someone who typed with only one finger.

Fr. Silva said a brief prayer. "Please Lord, help me find the right words to win over Mr. Berry." He made the Sign of the Cross and then began typing. His words flowed like thick syrup, and I cringed in frustration every time he hit a key. To make matters worse, he edited and edited to no end. At this rate, he'll never finish, I thought. I fell asleep, but then Fr. Silva woke me up.

"Is the letter finished?" I asked.

"I think so," Fr. Silva said. He looked cheerful but tired. He said writing the letter was more difficult than hammering out a sermon.

"This letter is fantastic," I said, reading it several times. "I think Mr. Berry will be impressed."

In the letter, Fr. Silva described El Lote as God's Garden for all to enjoy. In short, it said that over the years his property had fed many hungry families in times of need. Without his written permission, however, all that would end. "Let's hope Mr. Berry is a church going man," Fr. Silva remarked. After leaving the rectory, I dropped the letter in the mailbox and prayed that it reached Mr. Berry.

Weeks passed with no reply to our letter. Worried, I called Fr. Silva who came right over. Together, we mused over the letter's fate — maybe a postal clerk had misplaced it or delivered it to the wrong address. Then, it occurred to me that Mr. Berry might not be alive. Fr. Silva agreed and said that would explain everything. It now seemed unlikely that we'd ever get a response to our letter. Fr. Silva remembered that he had evening mass and excused himself. He'd be back later, he said.

Out of desperation I considered a nighttime raid to El Lote, but that would have been too risky. Red had been keeping the property under close surveillance and he'd surely catch me — I'd end up in jail. I even suggested buying nopales that came in a jar but Josefina flatly refused, remarking that they were too stale. With no other alternative, Josefina deleted nopales from the cafe's menu.

Days later, alone at the cafe, I heard T-Bird at the back door. "I've brought nopales!" he announced as he burst inside. Behind him were a legion of neighbors carrying bags and boxes filled with nopales. The line of carriers stretched to the alley, and even included children toting nopales in

Newspaper article about Oscar installing a new grease trap that reduced the flow of restaurant grease and ended the sewer problem at the shopping center. Press Enterprise. circa October 1984

small buckets. Apparently, T-Bird had gone around the neighborhood sounding the alarm about the cafe's troubles.

"How did you get all of these people to bring nopales?" I asked, startled by the multitudes.

"After hearing what happened at El Lote everyone wanted to help," he said.

Big Bertha, a close friend of Josefina's, had joined the crowd. "When I heard the news about the cafe, I borrowed this wheelbarrow and gathered up nopales wherever I could find them," Big Bertha shouted with enthusiasm. She told me she'd do anything to help my mom. "Josefina, out of the goodness of her heart, fed my family for two months after my husband lost his job," she said and promised more deliveries.

Others shared similar stories. One man, toting a gunny sack filled with nopales, said he wouldn't be here if it wasn't for Josefina. He'd paid a smuggler to get him across the border in Arizona, in the middle of the summer. "The greedy coyote (smuggler) unexpectedly raised the price and then threatened to leave me in the desert to die if I didn't come up with the extra cash. Your mother didn't hesitate to put up the money. She's a saint!"

Fr. Silva, when he heard the good news, rushed to the cafe. "I can't believe my eyes," he said when he saw so many bearing nopales. He said that God had answered his prayers, and blessed all those who were there. At that instant Red passed by in his patrol car, which drew loud jeers from the assembled crowd. Fr. Silva admonished them. "Please don't provoke him." When Red passed a second time, no one said a word or even looked at him.

The deluge of nopales ended after the last delivery. Green paddles flooded the kitchen — so much that it spilled into the dining room. I looked on with dread at the work ahead, since every paddle would have to be cleaned and sliced into small bits. Fr. Silva, not afraid of hard work, stayed behind to lend me a hand. We worked all night. When we finished, the cafe's nopal crisis ended.

The Mad Dog Tagger

Lupe hated cops. He regularly cursed at passing police cars, and once he even used an ice pick to puncture the tires of a police car parked in front of Carlos Market. So, I wasn't surprised when he suddenly began yelling at the two policemen sitting at the counter. "Mad Dog," he screamed repeatedly. Riled by Lupe's outburst, one of the officers told Lupe to shut up. But he wouldn't stop with his rant.

"Be quiet, or they'll kick your ass," I said, grabbing Lupe by the arm and dragging him into the kitchen. Dreadfully thin, he was no match for the two brawny cops with wooden nightsticks.

To my relief he calmed down. "I'm all right now," he said — his rage now almost completely gone. I apologized to the policemen. I told them Lupe was mentally ill, and that he wasn't a danger to anyone. The officers said they didn't care if he was crazy and warned me that if Lupe didn't settle down, they'd arrest him. Afterwards, I returned to the kitchen and quickly ushered Lupe outside.

I scolded him. "Lupe, you can't talk that way to the police." I reminded him what happened the last time he had a run-in with the police — they broke his arm and he ended up in jail for days because he couldn't find anyone to pay his bail.

"I'm sorry," Lupe said sheepishly, casting his eyes downward. He thanked me for helping him. He looked hungry, so I ran inside and got him something to eat. I told Lupe that the two policemen were probably done eating, so he'd better take his food and leave now; I didn't want them to find us in the parking lot. Lupe agreed and left.

With Lupe gone, I went back inside the kitchen. Chole, who'd worked at the cafe for the past year, met me at the door with a look of disapproval. "Why didn't you let the cops take him to jail?" adding, that at least behind bars he'd have a place to sleep and eat.

"The cops would have beaten him like a birthday pinata," I said.

"Maybe he needs a good beating. Besides, he's nothing but a freeloader," replied Chole. It was true, Lupe sometimes didn't pay, which infuriated the unsympathetic cook. I told Chole she should be more compassionate, especially since his meals weren't coming out of her pocket. "If you ask me, he's just plain loco and belongs in the nuthouse."

Not long afterwards pandemonium broke out in the dining room. "Someone just tagged two police cars in the parking lot," a customer yelled. The two officers, finished with their meals, promptly ran outside. I followed close behind. Using a spray can, someone had written "Mad Dog" all over their patrol car. Within minutes uniformed officers swarmed the cafe's parking lot. I'd never seen so many cops in one place; not even stabbings or shootings aroused this level of response.

The search for the tagger began in earnest. Officers went house to house, asking residents if they had seen who tagged the police car. As usual no one talked. Most people in the neighborhood didn't trust the police, which made it nearly impossible to get information. "I saw who did it, but I not telling the police shit," said a man in the crowd that had gathered to watch the excitement.

Tensions boiled over as the police scoured the neighborhood. I stayed out of sight; I didn't want to be around hostile cops who might think I had something to do with it. A few years ago, I witnessed a robbery and, wanting to be helpful, I gave a description of the suspect. He'd gotten away on foot. The detective who interviewed me said I wasn't being truthful: insinuating that I was an accomplice. Ridiculous, I thought. Why would I help rob a store and then volunteer information? From then on I stayed clear of the police. Then, unexpectedly, Chole came out from the cafe carrying a bucket filled with soap and water.

On her own, Chole began washing the afflicted patrol car. The paint was still fresh, so it didn't take her long to remove the offensive graffiti. Grateful policemen, who now seemed less edgy, thanked Chole and even offered her money, which she flatly refused. She'd returned to the cafe. I asked her what had possessed her to be so kind, since a cleaning crew had already been summoned. She answered that she knew Lupe was to blame, and what he did was disrespectful. "It was the least I could do."

After a while, unable to find the tagger, the police began to vacate the parking lot. They resembled a retreating army.

Officer Paz, known in the neighborhood simply as Paz, had stayed behind. Over the years he'd become a trusted family friend, and even attended my sister's wedding in Ensenada. He'd gone into the kitchen.

"Chole, you saved the day!" Paz exclaimed. She seemed embarrassed and told Paz it wasn't a big deal. "Nonetheless, I am grateful for what you did." Paz said that Chole deserved an award, but she brushed him off. He remarked that the chile verde smelled awfully good, and then glanced into the steaming pot.

Chole asked, "Are you hungry?"

"Actually, I haven't eaten all day," Paz replied.

"What about a couple of shredded beef tacos?" Chole suggested. "It'll just take a minute to prepare." Paz said that would be terrific and then turned his attention to me. His gaze wasn't a good-natured one, but a stern look he'd acquired from years of police work.

"Tell me the truth. Did Lupe spray paint those police cars?" Paz asked. Paz said that he'd heard about Lupe's earlier outburst in the cafe, which made him a prime suspect. Although Paz had seen Lupe in the neighborhood, he'd never met him.

"I'm not one-hundred percent sure, but more than likely Lupe did it," I said. Normally I wouldn't betray a friend. However, I trusted Paz. In fact, nearly everyone in the neighborhood adored Paz, who conducted himself more like a social worker than a policeman. In fact, unlike many cops who lived by the old maxim, "Shoot first, ask questions later," Paz often boasted that he'd never shot anyone. I couldn't imagine Paz taking pleasure in hurting anyone.

Right then Paz received a call over the radio. "Can't stay! I've got to go." He apologized for having to leave so suddenly.

"Don't worry. I'll keep the tacos warm," Chole said. He said not to bother. There was a shooting at a motel on University Avenue, and he'd probably be there for a long while.

The next day Paz returned to the cafe. He had disturbing news. Someone was spraying "mad dog" on police cars all over the neighborhood. Paz said that it had to be Lupe and asked me if I knew where he lived. "He's been homeless for years," I said.

"Didn't Lupe once live on Park Avenue?" Paz asked. I told him that Lupe's family had moved out years ago, and that the house was now vacant. Paz asked me if I'd go with him to Lupe's old house to look around. "I have a hunch he might be hiding out there." I agreed and we left together in his patrol car.

Once immaculate and clean, Lupe's former house was now run-down. Weeds and crabgrass overran the property and, to keep out squatters, every window had been boarded-up. Even the oak tree that Lupe's dad planted long ago looked sad and dry. "This was once the prettiest house on the block," I said.

We found the cellar door wide open. "Let's see what's down there," Paz said. We slowly walked down the wooden stairs, which creaked from years of use. It was dark and dusty down there, and a musty aroma loomed. Coke bottles and pizzas boxes littered the floor. "It looks like someone has been living down here," Paz remarked.

"Paz, look at what I found," I said. Amid the debris, I'd come upon a box that contained at least one hundred cans of spray paint. "Wow, there's enough here to tag every police car in Riverside."

"That settles it," Paz said. "This proves Lupe is guilty." Paz gathered the spray cans and put them in the trunk. To keep Lupe out, we nailed the cellar door shut. We even posted a no trespassing notice on the front door of the house. I commented that shutting Lupe out of his own house felt unfair, and it left a disagreeable taste in my mouth. Paz disagreed. He said the property now belonged to the bank. Lupe was trespassing.

Later that night, after the cafe closed, I heard footsteps in the attic above the kitchen. I grabbed the metal baseball bat that I kept in the kitchen and quickly ran upstairs to investigate. I heard someone calling my name. It was Lupe. Somehow, despite the wrought iron over the windows to keep out thieves, he'd managed to gain entry.

"What are you doing here?" I asked. Lupe said he didn't have anywhere else to go. Someone had nailed the cellar door at his mom's house, where he'd been staying; I didn't mention my role in this. He asked if he could stay a few nights. I said yes, but that he had to leave in the morning — I didn't want to risk the police finding him here. "The cops are looking for you. They say you sprayed-painted over a dozen police cars. Is it true?" He nodded his head.

"Please, don't call the cops. They'll send the dogs after me. Just like they did to my mom," he said, shaking with fear.

Lupe's accusations weren't merely the rant of a mentally ill man. Around five years ago, after stealing a pack of cigarettes from a local market, the police had followed him home. Afraid and confused, Lupe barricaded himself in his house. According to newspaper accounts, a trained police dog was sent in to flush him out. Unfortunately, the dog bit his elderly mother, who required stitches on her arms and legs — Lupe's father had died years earlier. Afterwards, Lupe told everyone he'd get even with the police.

I felt sorry for him. "I won't tell anyone," I said, even though I was skittish about harboring a wanted man. After all, the police had been looking everywhere for Lupe, even searching people's basements.

Afterwards, when Lupe simmered down, we reminisced about the old neighborhood. Lupe said he had fond memories of La Gran Fiesta Ranchera, and that in one of the game booths he'd won a goldfish, which sadly, he said, died the next day. He also recalled hot summer nights when he along with friends would sneak into Lincoln Pool and swim for hours. For a moment Lupe forgot his troubles. He smiled, and I almost didn't recognize him. It was getting late. Before I left, I warned Lupe to stay inside and to not make any noise. After all, he was a wanted man.

The next day I arrived early at the cafe. A crowd of people had gathered in front, and they were all looking up; I thought the building had caught fire. But it was Lupe. He was on the roof, gesturing and shouting obscenities at those below. "That guy looks like he's going to jump!" someone in the crowd cried out.

Minutes later, with horns blaring loudly, three fire engines pulled alongside the cafe. Lupe began shouting, "Mad dog, Mad dog." At times he ran along the edge of the roof; one misstep and he would have fallen onto the concrete below. This wasn't going to end well, I feared.

Fortunately, Paz was on duty that morning. He'd gotten the call and came right away. "Who's that on the roof?" he asked.

"It's Lupe," I said, explaining that I'd let him stay over-night in the storage room above the cafe, and from there he climbed to the roof. "I'm afraid he might jump."

"Don't worry, I'll get him down," Paz said. After some cajoling, he convinced the fire captain to let him use the fire truck's aerial ladder. When Paz reached the roof, I lost sight of him. I worried that Lupe would run and possibly jump off the roof when he saw a uniformed officer. However, I had faith in Paz. He'd find the right words to coax Lupe down. Finally, after an hour, the two of them suddenly appeared. Onlookers, many who recognized Lupe, applauded when he stepped off the ladder.

At Paz's insistence, Lupe wasn't handcuffed or questioned by the police. Instead, Paz ushered him into an awaiting ambulance, where paramedics tended to his cuts and scrapes. Afterwards, he was transported to a local hospital. I never saw Lupe again after that day. With both parents deceased and no relatives who could care for him, he most likely ended up in a mental institution. However, Lupe is still remembered in the neighborhood as the Mad Dog Tagger.

The Easter Curse

As usual on Easter Sunday, the cafe was packed with customers. Many had just left St. Mary's and eager to enjoy
a meal. It was the beginning to an auspicious day, until
Leroy, a mentally ill Vietnam veteran, began pounding
the dining room window with his fists. Terrified customers bolted. I raced to lock the main entrance door, but he'd
already entered.

I told Leroy to leave and blocked him from going any further. I didn't expect him to let my challenge go unanswered.
He lunged at me, but I stepped aside. He charged again, but
this time I hit him with a frying pan I'd brought from the
kitchen; he fell to the floor and lay groaning. I thought I'd
broken his ribs. Finally, he got up and stumbled towards the
door. Maybe he'd had enough, I thought.

Unfortunately, Leroy hadn't had enough. He just stood
there, gazing curiously at me. What happened next I
thought only happened in the movies: with his bare hands,
he wrenched the heavy door off its frame and slammed it
to the ground. Shattered wood lay scattered everywhere.
I wanted to run, but fear had immobilized my legs. In a
triumphal fury, he smashed what remained of the door. If
Leroy wanted to, he could easily have overpowered me and
ravaged the place. Instead, he bolted for the street and ran.

I didn't want Leroy to get away, so I followed him on foot.
However, I kept my distance which meant staying half a
block away. I'd heard about his three tours in Vietnam,

and that he'd belonged to a highly trained unit that killed and tortured people. Leroy's father lamented the army had turned his son into a monster who, without medication, was unfit to be around others. Once, in a dispute over money, Leroy stabbed his father. He served six months in county jail. After the incident, his family disowned him and since then he'd been living on the streets.

I followed Leroy to Lincoln Park. Minutes later the park swarmed with uniformed officers. I heard one cop comment, "Oh, it's him again. Better call for more backup." Leroy showed no fear and, at times, he even taunted the policemen who seemed nervous. When given the signal, eight policemen rushed him. Leroy went down without a fight and was quickly handcuffed. I was glad no one was hurt but baffled by his sudden timidity.

As the police led him away, Leroy launched into a bizarre rant. It was a chilling mixture of rage, prayer and black magic. One officer, clearly annoyed, jabbed his nightstick into Leroy's ribs to silence him. Now in the back of the police car, the prisoner turned towards me. "You'll pay for this, you fucking bastard," he shouted. If I had a mirror, I would have seen my skin turn sheet white. An officer standing nearby, who noticed my terror, told me not to worry. He said Leroy was going to jail for a very long time. Recently he'd attacked a bus driver, nearly killing him. Thank God for that, I thought to myself.

I returned to the cafe and found it deserted. The rest of the day only a trickle of food orders went out. I thought it odd since Easter was always busy. I closed early and I spent the rest of the day repairing the broken door.

The following year on Easter Sunday I expected to find a line of customers waiting by the front door for the cafe to open — as they had on previous Easter Sundays. The parking lot was nearly deserted. For hours I agonized over the drop in business. I couldn't understand what was happening. With no customers, I sent the kitchen staff home early.

Chole, a longtime employee, had stayed behind. She had urgent news that couldn't wait. "Someone's put a curse on the cafe," she announced. Chole explained that her neighbor, Tula, a well-known curandera in the barrio, had recently discovered the curse. Chole suggested that it was possible that this curse was ruining Easter Sunday business. If I agreed, she could make an appointment with Tula.

I didn't trust curanderas. I'd seen them prey on gullible people, who lost thousands to these charlatans. Even my own mother, a sensible woman, believed bad spirits existed and on occasion hired a curandera to protect herself and our family. However, I was desperate and was willing to try anything. "Could you arrange a meeting with her?" I asked.

"I'll call her right away," Chole replied. The next day Chole said she'd talked to Tula, who agreed to meet me as soon as possible.

To my surprise, Tula didn't look like a curandera. She wasn't old, decrepit nor wrinkled as I imagined. Rather, she seemed more like a perky soccer mom who spent her days carting children to and from games. "Glad to meet you, Memo. I hear you're in need of my services," she said.

"I don't want to seem disrespectful, but to be perfectly honest, I don't believe in evil spirits," I said. However, I admitted that I was up against something that seemed unnatural and unexplainable, and that I would be extremely grateful if she could help.

Tula turned dead serious. "I understand your doubts about my profession, but please believe me when I say your business is in danger." Tula said an evil entity had embedded itself inside the cafe and was bent on causing havoc. She'd discovered it while walking past the cafe. She asked me if anything unusual had recently occurred at the cafe, which could confirm the curse's presence.

Immediately, I thought of Leroy. I told Tula about the ruckus he'd caused and of his hair-raising rant that sent chills down my back. He might have been talking in tongues, I said, although I had no knowledge of such things. She listened intently. I went on to explain that since that day Easter Sundays were complete busts. "It's gotten so bad that I'm considering permanently closing on Easter Sunday.

Like a cancer doctor bearing bad news, Tula said, "I'm certain Leroy cast a spell on you that day." She said the curse at the cafe had the energy of a violent man, possibly a soldier. Tula's insights were uncanny, since I hadn't mentioned Leroy's military service. Whatever doubts I had about her vanished.

I asked Tula if she could get rid of the curse. She said curses were resilient but not unconquerable. A curse could last a few days or weeks, depending on its resolve. However, she stressed, it wouldn't leave on its own and had to be forced out. Adding, that removing this type of curse wouldn't be cheap. I asked the curandera how much it would cost, but she couldn't give an exact amount because every curse was different. I, nevertheless, hired her.

The following evening, accompanied by a legion of women toting Bibles, Tula arrived at the cafe. She explained that non-stop prayer was the best offense against a curse. It's like insecticide for demons, she laughed. They got right to work and formed a circle in the middle of the dining room. The cafe had already closed for the day, so they were alone.

Before starting the prayer session, Tula politely asked me to leave the room. My presence would be a distraction to the women, she explained. I retreated to my office, which adjoined the dining room but whose thin walls practically gave me a front row seat to the session. The assembled women mostly prayed but, at times, I heard loud cries and eerie shouts. Tula berated the curse, demanding that it immediately depart from the cafe. This continued for five hours. She finally adjourned the prayer session for the night.

The next day, in the middle of another session, a member of the prayer circle fainted. I expected Tula to suspend the session and send everyone home. Instead, this hard driving curandera said capitulation wasn't an option. After a short break the group continued; they prayed until the morning sunlight bled through the window blinds. With such vigor, the bad spirit didn't have a chance, I thought.

After two more agonizing days, Tula announced that she no longer felt the curse's presence anywhere in the building. "Prayer always triumphs against evil," she rejoiced. She thanked her helpers, who gathered their belongings and left. Tula looked exhausted. Her task completed, she said it was time to get down to business.

"How much do I owe you?" I asked.

She thought for a moment, and then said, "Nine hundred dollars should cover everything." Excessive, I thought. But if she'd indeed removed the curse, it was worth every penny. I asked Tula what guarantee I had that it wouldn't return. She said I shouldn't worry, since curses seldom reappeared in the same place. Furthermore, she assured me, "I guarantee my work. If the curse comes back, I'll come back at no extra charge." I handed Tula a check.

The following Easter Sunday I waited anxiously for customers to arrive. Chole, overly optimistic, had made enough menudo to feed the entire neighborhood. I'd even brought in more chairs and tables. And, just to make sure the curse hadn't returned, Tula gave the cafe a final cleansing. She declared the cafe curse free, and then hurried home to her family. Sadly, though, only a few customers showed up that day. Even the Sunday regulars from St. Mary's, exhausted and hungry after a lengthy Easter Mass, stayed away. With nothing to do, workers sat around in the kitchen. Thoroughly disgusted, I closed the cafe.

Afterwards, I realized that Tula had tricked me. The decline in Easter business at the cafe wasn't due to a wicked curse, nor was Leroy the boogeyman Tula made him out to be. I should have known better. Most likely, the long running Easter Sunday boon had simply run its course —fizzled out. In business school it's called Product Life Cycle. Simply put, customers were either eating at our competitor's, or eating at home with their families. There was no remedy. From that moment, the cafe never opened again on Easter Sunday.

Oscar's Retirement

Now fully retired, Oscar lived alone on his small farm. My mother, Josefina, had died years earlier, so there'd be no one around to help him if he fell or had a medical emergency. After a bit of coaxing, he agreed to move into the apartment above the cafe. This would have been impossible years ago, since the original cafe didn't have an upstairs. However, moving Oscar close to the family business turned out to be an existential threat.

Trouble first arose one Saturday evening. The cafe should have been buzzing with customers enjoying tacos and cold beer. Instead, the dining room was as empty as a beggar's wallet. With no meals to prepare, kitchen helpers had nothing to do. Pablo, the head cook, looked anxious. With a baby on the way, he needed all the hours he could get to pay for diapers and baby food. I told him not to worry but the sudden drop in business troubled me; I hadn't seen the restaurant this quiet since the Easter debacle.

I stepped outside to get fresh air. At the far end of the parking lot, encircled by thick smoke, Oscar was attending to a slab of ribs. Although he'd had a stroke a few years ago, which weakened his left side, he was now well enough to cook outdoors. He'd invited neighbors and customers over for ribs — free of charge, of course.

Rafael, a longtime customer, had joined the crowd. "Memo, your dad makes the best ribs in town," he said. For years he'd been eating at the cafe every Saturday. He always ate alone and drank Coronas until the cafe closed. Not surprising, Rafael was unsteady and slurred his words. I wondered where he'd gotten the booze, but then I spotted a metal tub filled with beer. Oscar, without telling me, had raided the cafe's stockpile of pricey Mexican beer.

Two hours later, when the last rib was eaten, people began to leave. Appreciative guests, that included children awash in barbecue sauce, thanked Oscar for his hospitality. He announced that he'd have another barbeque soon and promised to have hotdogs for the children. "You're all invited," he said. I cringed. I'd wrongly assumed that this barbeque had been a one-time event.

That evening I confronted Oscar. I said his barbecues were putting a financial strain on the cafe. Moreover, I pointed out, letting people drink beer in the parking lot was illegal; we could be fined or even go to jail. Worse, a drunk person could fall and the cafe would be held responsible. Oscar laughed and said I worried too much. After all, he said, the law specifically prohibited selling alcohol in the parking lot and not giving it away to appreciative guests. In his mind, he'd outsmarted the law. His carefree attitude infuriated me.

A week later Oscar borrowed a bigger grill, and once again neighbors and customers flocked to the parking lot to enjoy a free meal. If it hadn't been for the few customers who declined his offer, the cafe's dining room would been completely deserted.

This time Oscar had rented two big speakers, each capable of reaching every eardrum within a square mile. Luckily, the business next door was a sleazy massage parlor, and the manager was unlikely to call the police. People danced, drank, and ate with no end in sight. Then a police car pulled into the parking lot. Thank God it was Oscar's godson, Simon Lemos. He'd just joined the force, and he'd been assigned to this area.

Oscar warmly embraced Simon. "Mijo, come and join the party." Simon said he was on duty and couldn't stay. "Nonsense. You're not leaving without eating something." Out of respect, Simon didn't refuse — at our house, especially when my mother was alive, turning down a meal was an affront. As he ate, I noticed that he seemed uneasy. No doubt he'd noticed people drinking beer, and that some partygoers were intoxicated. Simon could have shut down the gathering, but instead turned a blind eye. He wolfed down what was left of his ribs, thanked his godfather, and left.

I closed the cafe. Oscar's barbecue had left no room for customers to park, so staying open would have been pointless. That night we had another unpleasant conversation. "Your barbecues are killing us," I exclaimed. "They have to end." He seemed truly sorry and promised never to barbecue at the cafe again. True to his word, the parking lot barbecues stopped. The usual Saturday business returned to normal along with profits.

With the business back on track, no one was more relieved than Pablo, who'd been looking for a second job. Sadly, though, Oscar became withdrawn. He watched television all day, and said he preferred to be alone in his room. He wasn't his old self. But Oscar couldn't remain a recluse for very long; it wasn't in his nature to shut himself from people. So, what happened next wasn't unexpected.

As before, Saturday night business plummeted. I went outside to investigate, expecting to find Oscar grilling. But there was no sign of him. No one had seen him or knew where he'd gone. I walked to Tony's Market; maybe he'd gone there to meet a friend or play cards with Tony. But he wasn't there either. I thought of calling the police, but decided to wait until I knew more.

Fortunately, I ran into Gordo. He was an old customer who'd stopped eating at the cafe after his second heart attack. Actually, Gordo would occasionally sneak into the cafe for menudo, a lethal breakfast for someone with advanced heart disease. He was in a hurry, and seemed annoyed that I stopped him. "Where are you going?" I asked.

"Your dad is throwing a barbecue at Lincoln Park. I'm headed there right now before it's all gone," said Gordo, struggling to catch his breath. He begged me not to tell his wife, who'd be furious if she found out. He was on a strict diet, and he wasn't supposed to eat red meat. I told him not to worry, and I promised not to say a word.

We finally arrived at the park. Every bench had been taken. It seemed the entire neighborhood had turned out for the barbecue, including many of the cafe's customers. Even the neighborhood winos took advantage of the free food. I wondered how Oscar had lured so many people to the park, but then I spotted a flier on the ground. It read: "Rib Fest At Lincoln Park." Oscar and friends had distributed them

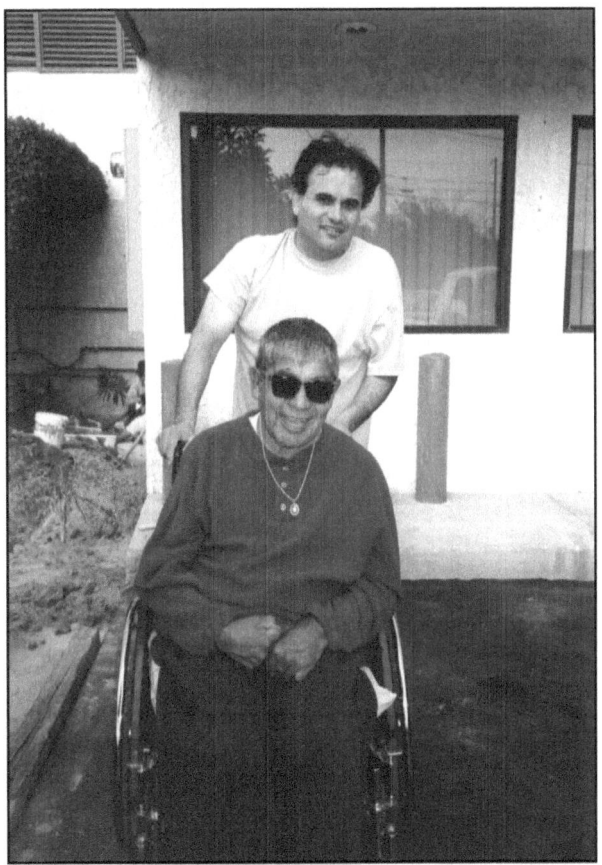
Bill and Oscar

throughout the neighborhood. However, I couldn't figure out how our customers, who didn't live in the area, had found out. This remained a mystery.

I didn't want to spoil Oscar's fun, so I watched from afar. Three hours later the last rib was eaten and people began to leave. Ben, along with the other winos, had volunteered for cleaning duty and filled every trash can. When we got to the cafe, I asked Oscar where he got the money to pay for the ribs; after all, they weren't cheap. He said that in the past few months he'd been saving his Social Security checks. And, to help offset the expense, Tony had sold him a case of spareribs at his cost. Neighbors also brought food, he said. I recalled seeing people eating potato salad and baked beans, which didn't come from the cafe.

It must have seemed peculiar for a restaurant owner to give away food, especially to his detriment. However, Oscar had lived through the Great Depression. He grew up poor and often relied on the kindness of neighbors for a meal. He never forgot this. As a result, he never turned away anyone at the cafe. Giving away a few bowls of beans wasn't going to break the business, he repeatedly said. Essentially, he had the heart of a soup kitchen operator.

If Oscar's rib feasts had continued, the cafe would have suffered real financial hardship. I could have insisted that he move back to the farm, but that wasn't a realistic option: although retired, he still had the last word about the cafe. I was in a tight spot, but then the solution came to me. After some cajoling, I convinced Oscar to return to work. Saddled with the duties of running a busy restaurant, he wouldn't have time to cook pro bono meals in the parking lot. And that's how the cafe survived Oscar's retirement.

Los Hallelujahs

One summer afternoon a rusted-out school bus pulled into the cafe's parking lot. A cadre of smartly dressed men and women disembarked and fanned out into the neighborhood, going door-to-door leaving behind leaflets. Oscar had been watching from his bedroom window and sent me to investigate.

I caught up to the fast moving solicitors. A spirited young man named Victor quickly stepped forward. He said they represented the Good News Ministries Church, and they were handing out invitations to tonight's services, for one night only. I asked, rather jokingly, if Catholics were welcome. Victor smiled and said everyone was welcome, no matter how they worshipped.

Victor asked me if I knew Oscar Medina, who owned a restaurant on University Avenue. He wanted to give him a personal invitation to tonight's services. I told him Oscar was my father, and that he lived in an apartment above the family business — I didn't mention that he'd retired. If he wished, I could take him there. Victor agreed. In a few minutes we arrived at the cafe. Oscar was downstairs, sitting under an oak tree that he'd planted years ago.

"Are you Oscar?" Victor asked. He seemed surprised when he saw Oscar in a wheelchair.

"Yes, that's Oscar," I interjected. I told Victor that Oscar had suffered from a stroke and was now a paraplegic. "He can barely talk and can't move any of his limbs," I said, pointing to his placid arms. Victor said he was sorry for my father's ill health, but then shifted the conversation to the business at hand.

Speaking directly to Oscar, Victor said, "My church is holding services tonight, and we'd like you to be our honored guest," — adding that he could arrange for a van to take us both, and then bring us back after the services. "The vans are brand new and super comfortable," he said, desperately trying to win him over.

At first Oscar seemed hesitant. His stroke had left him wary of strangers, and he seldom ventured out. I was sure he'd turn down Victor's offer, but then he bowed his head in approval. Victor thanked Oscar profusely. Before he left, in a lighthearted manner, he reminded Oscar not to forget to take his checkbook. He'd need it to write a big check.

I asked Oscar why he'd accepted Victor's invitation. After all, he was a devoted Catholic who disliked Mexican Protestants, especially Los Hallelujahs. Like other Mexicans in the barrio, Oscar viewed Los Hallelujahs as misguided Christians who worshiped in an undignified manner: screaming and acting out wildly in church. He brushed aside my question.

I called the phone number on the flier. In less than ten minutes, a van pulled into the cafe parking lot. It had a hydraulic lift for wheelchairs that Victor had ordered for Oscar. The driver was pleasant and offered us a bottle of water and fresh fruit. I wasn't sure if there'd be handicap restrooms at the services, so I politely declined. Since his stroke, restrooms had become a priority whenever we went out.

We arrived. The church, a massive canvas structure that resembled a circus tent, buzzed with visitors. Ushers escorted people to their seats. We recognized many of the worshipers: they were members of our local parish, St. Mary's. They pretended not to see us. I didn't blame them. An upstanding Mexican Catholic wouldn't be caught dead in a Hallelujah church. Like us, they were probably curious and bored, and hungry for adventure. We formed a tacit agreement to turn a blind eye to each other.

Victor finally caught up with us. "I'm glad you decided to come," he said, apologizing for being late. He had good news. He'd arranged for Oscar to participate in the Healing Hour, which was a blessing for the sick. Victor admitted that for a newcomer the healing session might be unsettling and that some people fainted: witnessing God's raw power could be frightening, he said. He asked Oscar if he had any objections. We looked at each other and Oscar said, "No." With that settled, Victor dashed off and disappeared into the crowd.

I hated to see Bible-toting hucksters use my father as a stage prop; surprised that he'd even agreed to take part in a religious scam. Maybe he hadn't heard Victor correctly, so I asked him again just to make sure he understood. "Once you get on stage there's no turning back," I cautioned. He nodded.

Moments later an usher escorted us to the so-called Gold Zone, reserved for generous donors. An attractive young woman brought us each a plate of chicken mole, a staple at Mexican weddings. Oscar said the mole was too watery, and tasted as if it came from a can. However, the attendants treated us well and constantly came around to refill our glass with iced tea. Victor had returned to make sure Oscar didn't have second thoughts about the healing session. I told him not to worry.

The sermon began when Pastor Eddie walked onto the stage. "Welcome everyone! Thanks for coming out to-night," he said. Pastor Eddie appeared ordinary and unim-pressive. He was short and stocky, and not handsome. He wore a navy-blue sports coat, which collided with his bright yellow slacks — obviously, he didn't pay much attention to fashion. I told Oscar that I didn't understand why he had so many followers. But I had underestimated him.

On stage, he cried, laughed, sang and even danced as he expounded on how Jesus died for our sins. Worshippers, in unison, waved their arms in the air, like people do at concerts when the music moves them. Some, overcome with emotion, dropped to the floor. Our priest at St. Mary's never generated such energy. In fact, I always struggled to stay awake during mass, especially at Christmas when mass lasted longer than usual. However, after a while, the sermon's intensity tired me. I was glad when intermission came, and he walked off the stage.

In preparation for the Healing Hour, Oscar and I were hustled to the edge of the stage along with others who'd been selected. I told him that it wasn't too late to change his mind. We could escape through an opening in the tent that I'd spotted earlier. But he insisted on staying. Pastor Eddie reappeared on stage and the Healing Hour began.

First in line was Rigo, who'd lost his eyesight to diabetes. He spoke into the microphone. "Diabetes has taken away my manhood. I can't work anymore or do the things I used to." He added that he felt useless, and said he'd contemplated taking his own life. Tears rolled down his face; he couldn't continue after a few minutes. Pastor Eddie abruptly cut in and embraced the shattered man. He promised Rigo that after tonight, with God's help, he'd be able to see again.

Pressing his hand against Rigo's forehead, Pastor Eddie cried out: "I ask in the name of Jesus, mend this man's ravaged eyes." Nothing happened at first. Undeterred, he uttered a litany of unintelligible words and phrases, which I'd never heard before. Seconds later Rigo said he could see a faint light in the distance. Pastor Eddie proclaimed that God, at this very moment, was healing Rigo's eyes. The crowd burst into a wild frenzy when Rigo turned towards them and announced that he could see again. He got on his knees and thanked the exhausted pastor. Afterwards, like a discarded stage prop, Rigo was hustled off the stage.

It was Oscar's turn. Pastor Eddie handed me the microphone. I'd never addressed a large audience before and was nervous. I began: "My father, Oscar Medina, had a stroke, which left him completely paralyzed. He struggles to talk, and that's why I'm up here. Doctors at the hospital said he would never walk again." The crowd let out a collective sigh. I went on to explain that he'd worked hard all his life; he even owned a successful business. "But the stroke had turned his life upside down. He'd become totally dependent on others. He can't even feed himself." Pastor Eddie put his hand on my shoulder, a gesture to let me know that it was his turn — I handed him the microphone.

"What do doctors know!" he screamed into the microphone. "With a strong dose of God's unfailing medicine your dad will walk home tonight — I guarantee it." He placed his hand on Oscar's forehead and, as he'd done with Rigo, beseeched God to restore his broken body.

Two men, who'd positioned themselves next to Oscar, lifted him in such a manner that he appeared to be standing on his own. Oscar hadn't been upright in years and looked nervous; at his age a fall could kill him. One of the attendants, sensing Oscar's apprehension, said in a low voice, "Don't worry, we won't drop you." The unsuspecting crowd roared with applause. Pastor Eddie bowed to the congregation like a magician who's pulled-off an impossible trick. Amid the commotion, Oscar was quietly lowered to his wheelchair and led to a dark corner of the stage where he couldn't be seen.

For the rest of the evening, we were kept hidden backstage. The church staff, for good reasons, didn't want anyone to see Oscar still bound to his wheelchair. After all, hadn't he just been cured in front of hundreds of eyewitnesses? When the crowd thinned out, Victor reappeared. He asked Oscar if he'd enjoyed himself and whether the chicken mole measured up to the cafe's standards. Oscar said he enjoyed it, but he was just being polite and didn't want to sound ungrateful.

Victor handed me an envelope marked "Donations" in bold letters. "I'm sure Oscar will be most generous," Victor said. He stood like a bellhop waiting for the obligatory tip.

I showed Oscar the envelope, but he refused to look at it. "What does he want?" he asked.

Hard of hearing, I shouted in his ear. "Money."

"Tell him I'm broke," Oscar said, which wasn't true — he got a check from the cafe every month, and he regularly donated to St Mary's. Victor's plastic smile suddenly melted away.

I reluctantly went along with the deception. I told Victor that Oscar lived on Social Security, and that he could barely afford his medications. "Sorry, but he doesn't have any money." I hated lying.

"I thought Oscar owned the cafe?" grumbled Victor, who glared at us, and threw up his arms in frustration and stormed off. I felt awful. After all, Victor had treated us well and even fed us. But my guilt didn't last long. Hadn't Victor used Oscar's disability for the Healing Hour? Hiring an actor would have cost the church much more than a dinner. In my mind, we were even. It was time to leave.

We waited outside for our shuttle. An hour later I spotted the driver who'd brought us. I told him Victor had arranged for a van to take us home. He looked at his logbook and said Victor had canceled that order. Besides, he said, all the shuttle vans were gone for the night. With no money for a cab ride, I pushed Oscar's wheelchair back to the cafe. I was tired, and a dog chased us part of the way. "I guess God punished us for pulling a fast one on the Hallelujahs," Oscar said sarcastically when we got to his apartment.

Ghost On The Balcony

This poignant story has become part of the cafe's lore.

The cafe was Carlos' first food delivery that morning. Oscar, the owner, would normally be inside tending to the menudo or counting money in the office. But he was running late and no one was there to let Carlos inside. He fretted that he'd have a long wait, a delay that would set him back in his deliveries.

A bitter cold battered Southern California that winter. Mornings were especially unbearable. To stay warm Carlos left the truck's engine running and turned-on the cab's heater. The hot air hit the young driver like a handful of sleeping pills. Carlos closed his eyes and he fell into a deep slumber. Then a swishing sound woke him.

On the balcony above the cafe's delivery entrance, an old woman was sweeping. She wore a headscarf but no sweater or shawl. At first, she didn't notice Carlos. Then, as if she could sense his presence, she glanced downward. Carlos waved at her, but she didn't wave back. She seemed annoyed by his presence and went back inside her apartment. Carlos had never seen her before, and wondered who she was. Most likely a tenant, he thought.

Carlos closed his eyes. With a newborn at home, he didn't get much sleep and rested whenever he could — even at work. A faint knock at the truck's door reawakened him.

He looked out and saw the old woman standing next to his truck.

Curious, Carlos quickly climbed down from the cab. The old woman had brought him pan dulce and a hot cup of atole. The atole would keep him warm, she said, telling him to drink before it cooled. He thanked her and explained that he was there to make a delivery. He was waiting for the owner to arrive to unlock the storage room. Carlos asked the old woman if she knew Oscar. She didn't respond.

Carlos apologized for the truck's loud noise, which he assumed had awakened her. The old woman replied that at her age sounds from the streets no longer bothered her; no apologies were necessary. He noticed that she had on a loose-fitting cotton dress. Her indifference to the freezing temperature outside baffled him since older people disliked cold weather. His grandfather, he remembered, always ran the heater at home, even during the summer months.

Inquisitive, Carlos asked the old woman how long she'd lived above the cafe. In a voice softened by advanced age, she told Carlos that she couldn't remember the exact year she moved in, but that she'd lived there a long time. He had more questions, but the old woman seemed hesitant to talk any further. She said goodbye and entered the stairwell that led upstairs.

The encounter with the old woman haunted Carlos. She seemed more like a vision than an actual person; though, the atole and pan dulce were real. The lights inside the cafe finally turned on. Oscar had arrived. He would surely shed light on the mystery.

Oscar apologized for being late. He had car troubles and had to wait for Buster Jones, a local mechanic, to tow his car to the garage. Carlos told him not to worry. He explained that while waiting he'd gotten a chance to meet the old woman who lived above the cafe. Oscar looked puzzled. He said out that no one lived upstairs — the apartment had been vacant for many years. "There's nothing upstairs except old dust and mice," Oscar laughed.

Stunned, Carlos insisted that someone did live upstairs. An old woman had come out on the balcony, he exclaimed. What's more, she'd brought him pan dulce and atole. The adamant driver stood by his story and offered to produce the pan dulce. Oscar, incredulous, suggested they go upstairs so that Carlos could see for himself.

After unloading the truck, both men climbed the staircase. It was dark, damp, and silent — utterly abandoned. A thick tangle of spider webs blocked their path, indicating that no one had been upstairs for years. Oscar said it was once an apartment, but no one had lived up here for years. Carlos looked around, sighed, and then told Oscar that he must have dreamt the old woman. After all, he didn't believe in ghosts. He thanked Oscar for his time. Carlos' detective work, however, had set him back even further in his deliveries. He wouldn't get home until late in the evening.

When Carlos returned to his truck, he found the pan dulce and atole resting on the seat where he'd left them. He couldn't believe his eyes. This was proof that he hadn't imagined the old woman. He wanted to show Oscar the pan and atole, but he couldn't spare the time.

The following year Carlos attended a family reunion. His sister, Lizzie, the family historian, had set up a display of family pictures. One photo caught Carlos' attention. He got closer for a better look. It was the old woman he'd seen at the cafe. Tia Carlota, another family historian, said that the woman in the picture was his great-great-grandmother, Ramona. According to family lore, Ramona was famous for her atole, and claimed that her recipe came directly from the mighty Aztecs.

Epilogue

As a historian, I felt an obligation to document Zacatecas Cafe's history. Since the business opened in 1963 it has been a large part of Riverside's Eastside community. Due to my father's penchant for politics and his gregarious nature, which we (including my siblings) inherited, the cafe didn't become just another Mexican restaurant that served tasty enchiladas and tacos. It morphed into a meeting place where homeless people, police officers, politicians, priests, blue collar workers, etc. all interacted inside a small space where anonymity was impossible. This combustion of people is what made the cafe a special place, and it provided the inspiration for my stories.

These stories, however, shouldn't be read as a memoir, which are true recollections of the past. The tales in *Cafe Stories* are fiction and intended to entertain readers. Yet they all contain bits and pieces of actual events and offer a glimpse of what I experienced at my family's small cafe.

About the Author

I was five years old when Oscar and Josefina opened Zacatecas Cafe in 1963. Along with my siblings (Suzie, Jon, Max) I grew up in the restaurant business. All four of us worked in the kitchen or waited on tables. And, all of us, except for Max, have managed the family business at one time or another. When my father died in 2002, I left the family business; Suzie managed the restaurant for a brief period. Jon, my brother, took over the cafe in 2005, and he along with his wife and children now run the eatery. I returned to school, and in 2008 I graduated with a Ph.D. in American History from the University of California, Riverside. Since then, I have been teaching history (adjunct professor) at Riverside City College and San Bernardino Valley College. I retired in 2022.

City of Riverside

Proclamation

WHEREAS, Oscar and Josefina "Josie" Medina opened Zacatecas Restaurant in November of 1963 at the corner of University and Park Avenues in order to serve the greater Riverside community and in particular the Eastside neighborhood; and

WHEREAS, the second generation of the Medina family continues to run the family business and maintain the same quality tradition of outstanding Mexican food and to provide a popular community gathering place for conversation; and

WHEREAS, thousands of people have enjoyed the warm family meals served over the past forty years by members of the Medina family; and

WHEREAS, in 1985, the business was relocated two blocks from its original site – to allow for additional dining space for the growing number of Zacatecas Café fans; and

WHEREAS, Zacatecas has grown not just in patronage but in reputation, beyond the borders of the City of Riverside; and

WHEREAS, Suzie Medina Hernandez is now running Zacatecas Café, recently taking over from her brother Bill Medina, and plans to continue the long history of this wonderful family restaurant for years to come;

NOW, THEREFORE, I, Ronald O. Loveridge, Mayor of the City of Riverside, hereby honor

ZACATECAS CAFÉ and the MEDINA FAMILY

for providing comforting food and warm conversation for the past forty years to residents and visitors alike and do give my best wishes for many successful and happy decades to come.

Ronald Loveridge

Ronald O. Loveridge
Mayor

November 20, 2003

Proclamation from the City of Riverside recognizing
the cafe for its years in business.

www.ingramcontent.com/pod-product-compliance
Lightning Source LLC
Chambersburg PA
CBHW050852180626
46814CB00007B/2743